Iceworld

Katherine Phillips

Copyright © 2011 Katherine Phillips

All rights reserved.

ISBN-13: 978-1456516321
ISBN-10: 1456516329

ACKNOWLEDGMENTS

This novel began as a creative writing project when I was in seventh grade, and after five years and several revisions, *Iceworld* has been developed into a fantasy fiction.

I definitely need to thank my family, my boyfriend, and everybody else for being so supportive of this book. Thank you to Mom, Dad, and Bernie, who were my editing staff, all the people who read my novel and gave me feedback, and every teacher who let me write so diligently in his or her class in my free time during middle and high school.

Chapter 1: Welcome to Iceworld

Mia Snow stared out the window and sighed. It had been snowing hard, without stopping or slowing, for the past five days. It was the middle of the winter, and no one had seen a blizzard like this for decades. Mia thought that winter was great, but she was fairly clumsy and kept falling, which was terribly unfortunate. She shifted her weight on the window seat so that her bottom didn't hurt so much from a particular fall earlier that day.

She stood and went to her bookshelf. It was packed with stories of brave people who had marvelous adventures in far-away places. Sometimes Mia wished she could just disappear and go on one of her own adventures. People in books always seemed to enjoy them so much.

There was a loud crash from downstairs. Her dad was having one of his fits. Since her mom died ten years back, he had been steadily losing his sanity. Each day was different: some were calm and normal, when he acted like he knew who she was and loved her; others were dangerous, and he usually shouted and threw things.

I'd better go and see what's up, she thought. There was a gut feeling that told her it would be safer to stay in her cozy, little room, locked away from any danger, but she felt responsible for her dad in the way a parent normally would for his child.

When she got downstairs, her dad was yelling incomprehensibly in a language that he probably didn't even understand himself. It was one of the worst fits he'd had in a long time. Mia would never call the cops. Instead, she normally just locked herself in her room and blocked the door.

Ducking as a rogue frying pan came flying in her direction, Mia screamed. She ran as it almost hit her. Without wondering whether it had dented the wall, she pulled on her boots as fast as she could and grabbed her coat. Her only goal was to get out the door and out of the way as fast as her legs would take her.

When she finally slowed down, Mia became aware of the light, pleasant breeze caressing her cheeks. *That's odd. The wind was practically blowing the window open before,* Mia realized. She looked around, slightly confused.

Nothing looked the same, and Mia saw with horror that her house wasn't behind her. She had never been lost before and had no desire to start now. Bitterly, she reminded herself that she had wanted an adventure in a far away land. "That just proves that I should be careful what I wish for," she grumbled to herself.

It seemed very likely that she was becoming as insane as her father, but it was just as likely that she had gotten lost. The thought that she might not get back home violently frightened her. She ran back the way she had come, hoping that her home was only just out of sight. No such luck. Deciding to head the way she had been going before, she hoped that she could find her way home or some help from there.

So, Mia walked. After a while her exposed skin started to burn from the feeling of the icy wind. Her breath became more and more labored, and her cheeks felt like they were on fire. She was beginning to think that she would never get home and wish that she had at least brought gloves or a hat.

Just as she thought she wouldn't be able to move her arms if she wanted to, Mia spotted a house a short distance ahead. She started running toward it stiffly. When she reached the door, she pushed her hair out of her face with numb fingers and knocked.

A short, plump woman swung the door open wide and looked at Mia for a moment with startled hazel eyes. She looked somewhat flustered, her mousy hair frizzy, her cheeks ruddy, and her old apron covered with flour smudges.

Then, gathering her wits, the woman exclaimed, "Oh you poor thing! Come in here now. You look as if the Ice Elves got you!" She ushered Mia, who didn't bother to ask what an Ice Elf was, inside. The woman took off Mia's coat and hung it near the fireplace and then ladled out some hot soup for the cold teenager, gently shoving her into a seat by the steady blaze.

Mia was more than happy to let this woman push her around. Since her mom had died, her dad wasn't really sane enough to care much about what she did, and it felt good to have a motherly figure fuss over her. "I'm Mia, um, Mia Snow," she told the woman, who was now stirring the pot.

The woman tasted the contents of the pot, rolling the soup around in her mouth a little, as if deciding whether it needed anything. Then, concluding that it did, she added salt. She brushed her short, dark brown hair out of the way and smiled back at Mia.

"That's such a pretty name. I'm Anna Grenville. My son, Ben, is just now joining us; he's probably be right around your age," she replied as a groggy boy in pajama pants came out, watching him with slight disapproval. His cheeks were tinged red and almost as bright as Mia's. He didn't look anything like his mother. Ben was tall, had deep brown eyes, and seemed like he went outside to do harder work more often. The only thing he shared with his mother was his dark brown hair.

"Wassdamadder?" Ben asked as he grabbed a bowl, his words slurring. Not seeming to notice Mia in his extreme tiredness, he started to spoon the hot soup into his bowl and proceeded to slurp it down without letting it cool. His mother shot him a disapproving look.

"Nothing's the matter, Benjamin, but we do have company. At any rate, you shouldn't slurp that down so fast," Mrs. Grenville added condescendingly. As soon as she had said it, Ben started coughing hard as it went down hot, fast, and in the wrong way. His mother came over and fussed over him, only to be brushed away.

Once she was sure her son was okay, his mother just smiled and stepped back. "There, see? What did I tell you? Finish your soup, get dressed, and come back here when you're lucid enough to speak with our guest."

Ben reluctantly obeyed, shooting his mother a bloodshot glare. While they were waiting for him to come back, Mia felt it couldn't hurt to ask a few questions. "How old is your son? Where are we? Can we call my house? I think my dad should be all right now, able to pick up the phone I mean." It all came out in a bit of a rush, sounding more garbled than she had intended. Instantly she turned red, feeling sheepish for having asked and revealed so much.

Mrs. Grenville stopped and dusted off her hands, seemingly untroubled by the mess of words that had been thrown together so hurriedly. "Well, Ben is eighteen years old, and our home is the farthest south that I know of. What do you mean, call?" Her brow furrowed in confusion as she asked her own question of Mia.

Mia panicked slightly, if there really was nothing south of here… that would mean that there was no home to go back to. "What? There has to be more to the south than this!" The feeling of panic welled a little in her voice, and she could start to feel her eyes prick.

Looking surprised, Mrs. Grenville answered, "No, I'm sorry; there is nothing to speak of beyond that small mountain range over there. No one is able to settle in the area there because of the wild animals and lack of building room. Why?"

"That's the direction I came from: home." Unsure what she could do, Mia started crying from the stress of an overwhelming situation. "What if I can't go home?!"

The older woman came over quickly and embraced her, folding the girl into her arms. She smelled of crisp seasoning and clean soap. "There, there, don't cry. Things are sure to get better soon. Just watch," Mrs. Grenville cooed to the sobbing girl, whom she held tightly.

It was very comforting to be held by this woman, getting her hair stroked and being shushed like a child. It reminded her of her own mother, when she was very small, holding her after a bad nightmare, whispering that it would be all right into her hair.

It was then that Ben made his reappearance, fully dressed this time. His cheeks weren't nearly so red but quickly went up in flame when he saw that a girl was crying into his mother's arms. He slowly backed out and waited for a few minutes until the crying slowed and then stopped. When he reentered, he studied the girl and saw that Mia's pale blue eyes were slightly red around the edges, but weren't swollen from crying. Her black hair framed her face prettily as she hung her head, gently staring into the bowl of cooling soup that she held in her lap. The sight of her struck him temporarily speechless; she was very beautiful and very sad.

Mrs. Grenville looked up and gave a small, tight smile to her son. Awkwardly, Ben walked the rest of the way into the room and sat down. Not knowing if he should say something, he asked, "So, uh, who's this?"

Mia looked up at him with her electric blue eyes. He tried to avoid her gaze by looking away. It was odd to feel so uncomfortable in front of someone in his own home.

"This is Mia Snow. She's lost her way home." Shaking her head slowly, Mrs. Grenville thought for a minute. Then she added, "I think you should take Mia to the capital, Ben. King Dimitri will be in Snowsdale, and he is the only one who might be able to send her back to where ever it is that she's from. Mia, you don't have any problem with that, do you?"

As Mia shook her head sadly, not caring what happened anymore, Ben blurted out, "But you've never even let me come with you to Telcrag! Now you're sending me all the way across Iceworld?"

"Not if you keep going on like that," Mrs. Grenville told her son coldly. That kept Ben quiet for quite a while as they started making plans for the trip.

"I can give you food to last for a while and then some money to stop and buy supplies when you run out," Mrs. Grenville explained after some time. "It'll be a long walk to

Snowsdale, but you may be able to get a ride from a merchant traveling north if you're lucky."

They continued to talk for a while about their plans for the upcoming days until Mia started yawning and couldn't keep her eyes open. Seeing this, Mrs. Grenville pounced on the chance to send them to bed.

That night, Mia wore a nightgown that she borrowed from the older lady, but once she laid down, she couldn't seem to fall asleep. In the middle of the night, she heard a scraping noise, as if a window was being opened, and she finally fell fitfully asleep, thinking of unwanted adventures and strange lands.

The next day was mostly for preparation. Near lunch time, when they were just starting to slow down, Mia pulled together her courage and asked a question that had been bothering her for a while.

"Where exactly are we?" Mia asked in a whisper, not wanting to seem foolish for not knowing.

Mrs. Grenville turned and stared at her for a moment before she realized that Mia was being completely serious. "This is the most southern territory of Iceworld. It is a land of snow. Greater cities are made of ice, and the capital in the far north holds a gleaming castle and the throne of the monarchs that rule over us."

Mia nodded, still unsure what that really meant for her. "So, Ben and I are going across your entire world to see the king of Iceworld? Will he be able to help me?"

"We hope so. If not, you're always welcome to come back here and live with us," Mrs. Grenville offered softly, patting Mia's cheek with a free hand. Mia nearly panicked all over again when she thought about how probable it was that she would have to take up that offer.

* * * *

Bustling around the morning after that, Mrs. Grenville packed all the last things that she thought could possibly help them out.

"Mom, I think we have everything," Ben said, exasperated, a backpack over his shoulders and standing at the door, head to one side and looking as if his eyes were going to come out of his head with frustration. When Mrs. Grenville stopped and gave him a look that made even Mia shiver. Ben unconsciously withered under his mother's glare. "Um, never mind," he muttered, stepping back.

Mia ducked her head so that the two wouldn't see the smile that had involuntarily crept across her face. It was funny to see him crumble as he had from a single look. Laughing silently, she looked up to see Mrs. Grenville moving around again with Ben purposefully avoiding his mother's glare.

Not much longer after that, they set out on their way to Snowsdale. They started following the Slippit Road; it was supposed to lead all the way to the capital. Mia was somewhat discouraged that the entire road seemed to be made from a slick ice. It certainly was going to be a long and arduous walk to the capital.

* * * *

"Aaaaahhhhh!" Mia's scream rent the air yet again; her voice was starting to go a little hoarse. Landing hard on her backside, she glared up at Ben, who had stopped to look at her and was fighting a losing battle to hide his laughter. "Aren't there any roads that *aren't* made of ice?"

The tall boy pretended to think over her question a minute, a smirk on his face, before replying shortly, "No." He was laughing lightly. "You know, we would get there a lot faster if you didn't keep falling all the time." He looked at her pointedly and tried not to notice how flushed her cheeks were.

"Sorry, it's not like I try to," she snapped. Suddenly remembering something, she added, "Although, the last time wasn't so bad." She had fallen into the snow and made a snow angel for fun. The surprise came when she stood up, followed by the angel before it flew away! It was one of the most amazing things she had ever seen. She hadn't been sure if it was normal or just as magical as she thought, and so kept quiet about it. Looking after the angel, she had wondered how it had happened or if Ben had even seen it. Mia didn't want to seem stupid, but she couldn't help asking, "Did you see that?"

Ben had kept walking and said, "No," flatly and distantly without turning around, as if he had been thinking about something else all together. Mia had kept quiet after that, not wanting to bother him. He not only seemed easily bothered, set off by the littlest things, but also impervious to some of the things that might bother her.

Presently, Ben started walking again, pulling Mia out of her reverie. "You won't have to keep falling down forever. I think I've got an idea that could get us there *so* much faster." He shot her a look, his voice dripping with sarcasm.

"Hey!" Mia protested, only a little offended; she knew it was true.

Ben laughed more lightheartedly than she had heard yet. "Just follow me." With that said, he stepped off the icy road. Mia was surprised but followed without complaint; she'd do anything to stop slipping on the hard ice. "Where are we going, Ben?" she asked, jogging to try and keep up.

He turned and looked at her as if she were stupid, a hint of a grin on his face. "I thought you knew that," he said, his voice mocking her. Mia shook her head, feeling as if she was missing something and that it was obvious that she didn't know, or she wouldn't have asked. "We're on our way to Snowsdale so that you can get home," he said sarcastically, his grin breaking wide across his face.

Mia frowned at him, her confusion dissolving into annoyance. "Oh, ha ha. *Really* funny. I'm not that stupid, Ben. I meant, where we are going for the faster way to Snowsdale?"

Ben just smiled cryptically, "You'll see. I'm sure you'll like it though." With more than slight annoyance, Mia blew her hair out of her face and grudgingly followed him. In the distance, she could see the hills looming tall in front of them.

Ben led her farther and farther away from the road. Not really caring where, Mia wanted to rest; her legs felt like lead, cold lead. They had been walking for a long time, and it didn't look as if they were stopping anytime soon. They had almost reached the hills, and Ben was headed toward the tallest one out of them all.

"No way, Ben. If we're going up that thing, we're resting first. I never went walking back home. I'm not used to this kind of thing," she told him. She thought it best to tell him that she wouldn't make it half way up the hill.

"Don't worry, Mia. We're not climbing that hill. That would be ridiculous." He rolled his eyes dramatically and shook his head. "No, we're going into it." Ben kept moving towards the hill. Wondering what he meant, Mia followed as fast as she could, stumbling slightly in the powdery snow.

When they reached the foot of the hill, Mia saw that there was a large opening of a tunnel nearby. Ben started inside without looking at her, so he didn't get to see her apprehensive expression. Mia reluctantly followed, resenting that she had ever once set foot out of her house two days ago. The tunnel was dark and seemed to go on forever. They walked on and on in pitch darkness. Mia was just about to ask how much farther they had to go when the tunnel opened up onto an enormous cavern that was dimly lit by burning torches on the walls. It was luxuriously furnished with piles of thick, lush rugs and tapestries. The rest of the cavern was strewn with fabulous gems and jewels, gold goblets and plates, even necklaces and bracelets. "Oh, my gosh! Ben, how did all of this stuff get in here?" For a instant Mia was absolutely and completely dumbstruck. This was the last place she ever expected to find a hidden treasure hoard. Then she added sharply, "And I don't see any way to get to Snowsdale quickly, unless there's a flying carpet in here somewhere."

"Don't worry; I didn't steal any of it. I found the cave a while back, and all of this stuff was in here," he reassured her. "And no, there's no flying carpet. Look, you'll see the ride that we've got in the morning, because it's getting late. You should rest. I'll wake you up in a few hours." He walked off unceremoniously, leaving Mia to make herself comfortable. Mia lay down on the rugs, curled up, and fell asleep.

Chapter 2: Nomis

Mia yawned and sat up, looking around at the dimly lit cavern. As she awoke, it felt as if she was the only living thing in the world. There was no sign of Ben anywhere.

"If this is a joke, I am going to hurt Ben. This is so *not* funny," Mia said. Where was he? Sitting still and waiting impatiently, she held her knees to her chest and studied the cavern around her. Large gouges covered the walls in odd formations, looking as if something enormous had drawn its claws across them. The sight of them and her imagining what kind of animal could do that made Mia shudder, and she then forced those thoughts out of her mind.

Fifteen minutes passed, and there was still no sign of Ben. Getting up, she pulled out a little bit of bread from her pack. It had been a long time since she had last eaten, and she was ravenous. She thought it better not to waste their supplies, though it seemed like they should be able to bring some of this hoard with them to pay for more as they needed it.

Almost an hour later, she heard Ben's voice; he was talking loudly, but no one was responding. There was a loud rumbling sound coming from the same direction as his voice, and it sounded like they were both getting closer. Confused, Mia stood up. "Ben?" she called cautiously. Ben came running into the cavern, eyes wide.

Looking somewhat worried about something, he glanced back at the mouth of the cave before crossing to her and talking her arm in his hand. He had a very firm grip. His hands were calloused, but Mia decided against concentrating on that. "Mia, whatever you do, don't freak out, okay?" he asked of her in slow tone that worried her. His eyes were locked on hers, pleading her to stay calm. "The... uh... thing... that's going to come in might look scary, but I promise that he won't eat you." The hesitation frightened Mia more than anything else had yet.

"Who is it? Better yet, *what* is it?" Mia asked, trying unsuccessfully to keep the edge of panic out of her voice.

Ben caught the sharp edge in her voice easily. "Don't worry; you'll see." He turned to the mouth of the cavern and whistled sharply, a high, piercing note. Mia clapped her hands over her ears momentarily to protect them from the painful sound.

The rumbling grew louder yet, and added to it was a scraping of nails on stone. Then, from the cave's entrance, came first the head and neck of what looked like an enormous serpent. Next came a large, scaly foot, quickly followed by the other, as well as shoulders, wings and the rest of an enormous dragon. It was the color of ice with a tinge of blue on each of the glimmering scales. On the wings and the beast's brow were jagged, icicle like spines. The whole dragon had an air of regal majesty, and for a moment, Mia forgot to be afraid, caught up in the sheer brilliance of this beast, but only for a moment.

Ben looked nervously at Mia for her reaction. Her jaws were locked together and her eyes were wide with fear. She didn't move once, except for her eyes, which were now following the dragon as it came closer and lay down beside her. "His name's Nomis. Mia, I promised he wouldn't eat you, and he won't. Really. So, just calm down and do something so that I know you're not dead," he joked half-heartedly. "My mom would kill me if you died." He hadn't really been surprised by her reaction to Nomis. She *was* the first person he had shown, or told for that matter, but the reaction wasn't unexpected.

Mia took a breath and nodded at him, her eyes still wide. She noticed that all of Ben's things were still packed and that they were sitting next to a leather harness, which looked as if it were designed for a purpose. Suddenly, suspicion overwhelmed her. She hoped she was wrong but wasn't asking, just in case.

Nomis eyed her from his resting spot. Mia realized that she had been on his bed a few minutes ago as she stared into one large eye. It was deep and piercingly bright blue. Mia's own eyes were a slightly mistier tint of blue.

Ben grabbed his pack and gestured in Nomis' direction. "He's our way to Snowsdale. We'll get there a lot faster riding him than slipping and falling."

Staring open-mouthed at him, Mia realized that she had been right and regretted it. Plus, it wasn't as if she *tried* to fall all the time. It hurt! As far as the flying went, she wasn't too disconcerted. She wasn't a big fan of heights, but she never had a problem flying when going on vacations with friends. Then again, she had never been on a dragon's back while flying before. The idea made her slightly anxious and even a little nauseous.

Ben began grabbing their things and carrying them over to Nomis already, letting her process the information. Mia watched him tie the packs together and sling them over the creature's back before patting him on the shoulder. With a huge shock, a realization hit Mia. This wasn't just a means to travel quickly or even a beast that Ben had befriended; it was his...no, could it?

"He's your *pet!*" Mia exclaimed incredulously. "I can't, and won't, believe that your mom would just let you raise a dragon!"

Ben looked up at her carefully, slowing his tying of knots, and shrugged. "Then don't. Mom doesn't know about Nomis, not yet anyway. But she will when I come back home on him, won't she?" The indignant question answered itself.

Mia's face went from slightly shocked to reluctantly understanding. "Yeah, I guess so, but didn't she notice when you sneaked off?" Mrs. Grenville didn't look like she would miss anything bigger than a sneeze from her son.

"If you asked my mom about me, she would probably tell you that, as a teenager, I sleep a lot. Whenever I pretend to be asleep, she leaves the room, and then I jump out the low window in my room. One day I got lost and found this huge cave with all these things in it, including a baby dragon, Nomis. I come to see Nomis whenever I'm sure my mom's not looking out the kitchen window." The dragon looked around at the sound of Ben saying his name. "Now I see him all the time." The love and pride that was emanating from Ben's voice was a result of many years together; Mia could tell without asking. She smiled lightly at the explanation.

Ben looked around the cave, clapping his hands together. "Well, I think we're ready. Climb on." He did so and waited for Mia to do the same, looking at her expectantly.

Mia, meanwhile, was still a little unsure about the whole flying thing, but she didn't want Ben to know that Rather, she wanted to seem brave, as if she was daring enough to try anything. She climbed up rather ungracefully and sat behind him.

At a signal from Ben, Nomis stood and walked toward the mouth of the cave. "Are you positive this is safe? I've never done this before," she told him, her anxiety was easily revealed in her voice.

Ben just nodded. They had reached the tunnel now and had started going back outside. The trip *out* of the hill seemed a lot shorter than the one coming in, which didn't necessarily seem like a good thing to Mia. When the dragon got outside and into the open air, he reared up on to his hind legs and started to flap his wings, stirring the air around them, preparing to take off.

Mia grabbed Ben tightly around the waist and didn't let go. Ben just smiled. He didn't dare laugh and have her let go and fall off. It was easy to tell that she was frightened, though she *had* tried to seem brave. Instead, the terrified girl was clinging onto his waist as if her life depended on it before they had even taken off.

Mia didn't find it in the least bit funny. She had never done anything like this, and at the moment she didn't care for it at all. It was nothing like getting on a plane. Planes were more comfortable and less likely to drop their passengers. When Nomis took off, Ben hollered and swung his arm into the air animatedly, nearly unsettling Mia right behind him.

The dragon's wing-beats soon became steady, and the trip was a lot smoother than she imagined it would be. After a while, the up-down rhythm of Nomis' wings felt almost calming. It turned out to be a very long trip for the day, though. They stopped only for short periods of time at once and then kept going.

The only time that Mia dared to loosen her grip, Nomis promptly flapped his wings, and Mia, who hadn't quite gotten her balance yet, swayed dangerously and grabbed Ben again. She soon decided that she hated heights and chalked it up to it being a bad fear. Unfortunately, it seemed like one that she'd have to get over quickly.

Eventually, she did let go of Ben and went to clutching onto one of the dragon's spines as if her life depended on it. Once the sun started setting in the western sky, Ben directed Nomis to land, and they stopped in a valley that had an outcropping of rock, large enough to cover the three of them, to give them enough room to lay out sleeping bags, and to start a fire for dinner.

Once they put some melted snow in a small pot above the fire they had built and added some crucial ingredients, they soon had enough stew to feed the two of them for the night. It was salty and had a flavoring that had seeped from the meat they had put in it.

Ben stirred the stew in his bowl slowly and thoughtfully. His brown eyes glinted in the firelight as he looked into the flame, pondering something. "What's your family like, Mia? You've already met mine," he asked suddenly, his manner more light-hearted than she would have guessed. Mia gave him an incredulous look. He grinned, "Just asking."

"Two things: First, that's a personal question, and it's rude to ask. Second, it's really none of your business, Ben," was her only response. Ben felt as if he had been slapped and dropped it without pressing for any more details.

Mia wasn't sure why she didn't tell Ben that her mom had died nearly a decade ago and since then her dad had gone almost completely crazy for some unknown reason. During his sane moments, he assured Mia that it was neither of their fault that her mother was dead, but sometimes she wondered. She herself had been a total mess since she had started having those thoughts, and no amount of counseling helped her.

When they finished eating, they unrolled their sleeping bags and crawled in. They fell asleep soon, Mia thinking about her mother and what she had gotten herself into, and Ben thinking about why Mia had gotten so angry, how to get her to open up, and what was to come on this strange journey they were only just beginning.

Chapter 3: Tancredo

    The next morning Mia awoke to the soft, low grumbling of an animal. With a start, she sat straight up and looked around in a panic, having had dreams that were full of snarling beasts and sharp teeth. Seeing that it was only Ben snoring softly and deciding that next time it would be a harder object, Mia threw one of her gloves and hit Ben square on the back of his head. Merely rolling over, Ben tucked the thrown glove under his chin like a child with a teddy bear.
    Mia chuckled; she had never met anyone who slept as deeply as Ben did. She got out of her bedroll and looked out at the glimmering snow. Between Nomis's scales and the new snow, it looked like there were diamonds scattered everywhere. Mia stood still for a while, just watching the lights glimmer and dance, caught up in the beautiful moment that she didn't have to share with anyone in the world.

Ben started to wake up, feeling a shift in the surroundings as Mia moved about. When he sat up, he found Mia's glove in his sleeping bag. Wondering how it had gotten there, he looked around and spotted Mia. Facing away from him, Mia's black hair cascaded down her back, shimmering in deep contrast with the pure white snow around her. Snapping himself out of the minor trance he'd been lulled into, he threw the glove back at her. He missed and the glove went sailing past her. Mia saw the glove land nearby and turned around to laugh at him. Ben just laughed back at her. He had to admit that it *was* kind of funny.

Mia started making breakfast, plain oatmeal, wincing as she bent over.

Ben smiled. "Sore?" He was only half asking; he knew what the answer would be.

"Yeah. Aren't you?" Mia was surprised when he shook his head in response.

"I was my first time, but I'm so used to it now that I don't get sore anymore." Ben's comment made Mia wonder how many times he had ridden the dragon before. She decided that it wasn't worth asking.

Nomis rose to his feet, stretched, moved away and took off, flying out of sight before Mia could even open her mouth. Mia looked after him, alarmed. "Where's he going?" If the dragon were gone, that would mean that they would have to walk the rest of the way. Weighing the options, she mentally shrugged. She would end up with a sore bottom either way, it seemed.

Ben looked up at her, unconcerned, and then grinned faintly at her worry. "He's not leaving us here; he's just going to go find something to eat." He spooned the breakfast from the pot into his bowl and then started eating it immediately. "Nomis needs to eat, same as we do. Now sit down and get some before it's gone." Ben spooned more oatmeal into his mouth.

His comment having reassured her, Mia sat and raised an eyebrow at him. "You shouldn't stuff that much food into your mouth. Remember what happened last time?" she asked. She had barely gotten the words past her lips when he gagged on the large amount of porridge. Mia started to laugh. "See? What did I tell you?"

Ben narrowed his eyes at her. "Oh, don't rub it in," he said faintly through coughing. By the time they finished breakfast, Nomis had returned and was waiting patiently for them to pack up.

They tied up their bags and bedrolls and slung them onto Nomis's back, securing them as tightly as they could manage. After mounting the scaly beast, they flew for hours before resting for lunch. The two of them chewed slowly; now even Ben's legs were sore from being on the dragon so long and neither was eager for more flying so soon.

Suddenly, the hairs on Mia's neck stood on end. It felt as if someone or something was watching them. A shiver ran up her spine as she looked around. Nothing was there. She kept looking over her shoulder while they were on the ground, for the feeling didn't go away for some time.

When it finally did, Mia relaxed slightly and surveyed the ground around them. There were small footprints everywhere. Then, out of the corner of her eye, she caught a flash of movement. Looking over sharply, Mia saw the food sack running away!

She yelled and lunged after it. Ben looked over and ran after it. "It's the Ice Elves!" he called, diving after it. The bag barely slipped out of his fingers. The Ice Elves were getting away, and then they and the bag disappeared.

"Stupid imp," Ben mumbled darkly, getting to his feet.

He checked their extra bag. They had little food stored in there. "We have to find a city soon. We only have enough for tonight and tomorrow with this bag."

Mia nodded glumly. She wasn't very hungry and tucked what remained of her sandwich back into its little wrapper. "Where is the closest town?"

Ben thought for a minute, trying, in vain, to calm down. "Well, I think we're too far east for Telcrag, so I'd say Tancredo is the closest. It should be a little northeast of here."

Mia glanced at Nomis, wondering how fast he could fly. "How long?"

Ben shrugged, still in his murderous temper. "I'm not really sure. I've never been this far north. I'm going to guess around a day and a half.

Mia sighed. "Then we might as well get going, especially if that's all the food that we have left." She grabbed the remaining bag and tied it to Nomis as best she could.

Ben nodded. "You're right; let's go." After helping tie the bag more securely, he jumped onto Nomis, wincing as his sore legs rubbed against the hard scales. Mia got on too, but slower and more carefully so her pain wasn't as pronounced as his.

They set off quickly. That night when they stopped, it was by the edge of a river. Mia looked at the water rushing by and argued with herself over the possibility of taking a bath and how cold it would be. Looking over, she saw that Ben was already peeling his coat and scarf off.

Bright red, she gaped at him as he paused and shrugged. "Do you mind? You can wait on the opposite side of Nomis, can't you? You can have your turn later and maybe start a fire while you're waiting?" He was hoping she wouldn't argue with him. Mia didn't even think of arguing. She rounded the form of the resting dragon and untied the remaining pack. She pulled out the lighting stones and started to work on the small bit of wood that they had with them.

Hearing Ben's shocked gasp from the shallows of the icy river, she struck the two stones together and cursed as again and again she tried with no luck whatsoever. She sat fuming over the small pile of wood, wishing it would light itself. In a fit of frustration, Mia threw the stones at the dry pile of wood.

It was then that Ben came around Nomis, fully clothed. Mia straightened up, her face red with anger and humiliation at not being able to do one of the simplest things of their journey. Ben stared past her for a moment and then smiled widely. "Good job getting the fire started," he commented brightly.

Mia scowled at him and glanced at the pile of firewood. Surprised, she looked again and saw a blaze now steadily eating away at the wood. Stunned into silence, she tried to figure out in her mind what must have happened. "But it wouldn't light," she muttered.

Ben turned and looked at her, his expression indicating his confusion. "Well, apparently you got it to work," he replied, gesturing at the flame. "Obviously," the gesture indicated. Mia rumbled darkly and finally decided that the stones had sparked when she'd thrown them down.

"I'm going to go take a bath now. I'll be far enough to the right that I won't be able to see you or the dragon," Mia informed Ben curtly. "Don't think about coming after me."

Ben's mouth dropped open and his ears turned red. "Why would I want to?" he asked indignantly.

Mia shook her head and walked alongside the river until she couldn't see the other two or anything else that would disturb her privacy. She peeled off her many layers of clothes and got into the freezing water before the wind had a chance to get her.

Shock rippled up her spine, causing her muscles to lock up. As quickly as she could, she rubbed the water onto her arms and body and clambered back onto the bank, reaching for her clothes.

Safely bundled up again with teeth still chattering, she made her way back to the camp. Her hair was still drenched but pulling the hood of her heavy coat over it helped protect her against any passing breezes that would only worsen the cold experience of being wet.

Ben smiled grimly at her when she got back and handed her some of the dwindling food. There was no food to cook over the fire, but both Ben and Mia huddled as close to it as they dare.

The next morning came and went, and soon it was past noon. Just as Ben had predicted, they reached Tancredo in the late afternoon, still long before the sun would set. They had Nomis wait on the small stretch of land before they came to Tancredo's gates and headed toward the city.

As they got closer, Mia couldn't help noticing how the ice walls made the city shine in the sun and lights bounce off them.

Ben stared at it curiously, seeming confused by something. "Only cities and large towns have ice buildings. Other places, like the closest town to home, don't. You need a lot of people to make a crystal city; otherwise wizards spend a lot of time working on something that never is seen by anyone who won't take it for granted. I don't know why Tancredo is; it seems way too small," he explained as they got closer. Shrugging, he smiled as Mia adopted her own puzzled look. "The walls never melt because they're reinforced with magic. You can't see in or out through the walls so everyone still has their privacy. It takes a lot of a wizard's energy to reinforce ice into an opaque crystal that isn't cold to the touch."

Mia nodded, looking at the crystal-city in amazement. The closest thing she had ever seen to that was a picture of the big cities, but those were of tinted glass, not crystal or ice. She wanted to go and take a look around before they left, but she debated on whether Ben would let her.

When they entered Tancredo, it seemed like the villagers were content, if not truly happy. They knew each other and greeted and waved to people passing, but there was a certain strain in their faces and smiles. In their past they had suffered some loss. It was written on all but the youngest children's faces.

"I'll buy the stuff," Ben offered. "You can go look around if you like." He walked off into the crowd of noisy villagers. Excited by the chance to explore, Mia set off in a different direction.

Mia wandered around, looking at different vendor's supplies and trinkets. Some were very beautiful, and she didn't even know what other ones were. She kept walking and soon found a quiet area of the city that was seemingly deserted except for a few small children running around, but even they disappeared after a time.

Wondering what was back there; Mia kept walking through the alleyways and soon came to a large wall. It was so tall that there was no way she would be able to see over it, and as far as she could see, the wall didn't end in either direction. Instead it curved on both sides, as if to form a circle. There wasn't a door, but there had to be an end to it.

Mia walked left along the wall, hoping to find some sort of break in it. She kept following it. Soon she thought there appeared to be more activity, but she had just made a complete circle and ended up back where she started.

Sighing in disappointment, Mia looked a little more carefully at the wall. She spotted a small design of swirling lines that formed the shape of a hand. Walking forward and looking at it a little more carefully, she felt as if an invisible string was drawing her toward the design.

Now why is that here? she thought. Mia took off her glove and felt the lines on the mysterious wall. They were worked right into the wall so that she couldn't even feel any ridges with her fingers, even when she pushed her palm against it as well, resting her whole hand on it. Strangely, the wall wasn't cold. Ben's words from earlier came back to her, and she remembered that he had said that the walls in ice towns were reinforced with magic and wouldn't betray any ice-like qualities.

All the same, she still wanted to know what was behind that wall. Suddenly, a huge tremble shook through her body. A small fissure ran up the length of the wall, creating an extremely straight line on it. She stepped away quickly and pulled her glove back on, her eyes growing wide with horror. The wall trembled again and parted down the seam of the crack. Soon a large gap stood before her, showing a vast and expensively furnished room beyond. Joyful-sounding bells pealed through the air, making Mia jump and look around, scared. She ran back into town and found Ben as the village stared at her dashing by.

Locating him, she grabbed his arm and spoke to him in a rushed whisper as the villagers gathered around them in a circle. "Ben, something happened. I don't know what it was, but I think we should get out of here." She glanced over her shoulder worriedly at the surrounding people. Huge mobs were usually something to be nervous about. "Ben, let's go!" she pleaded, yanking him by his arm.

"Oh, you won't be going anywhere," a low voice purred, obviously pleased by the chance to use authority. A tall, robed man stepped out of the crowd. His robes were a deep purple with gold lining around the hem, cuffs, and neck, and he looked very official and cold-mannered as he sneered down his nose at them. "It's only good manners that you tell us who you are first. And where are you going in such a hurry would be very nice as well." Something about his tone implied that it wasn't a mere suggestion.

"This isn't good," Mia whispered, not really directing it at anyone. She felt like she was going to be sick to her stomach, and she closed her eyes.

"Really, Mia? I had no idea," Ben replied sarcastically so quietly that only she could hear. "I shouldn't have just let you go around town. Let me do the talking. Knowing our luck, you'd only make things worse." Mia opened one eye and scowled at him and watched as he addressed the robed man. "We're on our way to the capital, Snowsdale. An Elf stole most of our supplies, and we were hoping to restock here."

Ben's smooth and truthful words, however, didn't help them. The robed man simply glared at them and said coldly, "So you thought to take your 'supplies' from the Royal House of Tancredo? I very much doubt that you are telling the truth." A constant smirk at the corner of his lips threatened to overtake his entire mouth. Mia particularly disliked this man and fought the urge to say something that would get them into trouble.

"We weren't breaking into anything. We didn't even know there *was* a Royal House in Tancredo," protested Ben.

His temper was rising now, and he kept closing his eyes in fits of exasperation and frustration. Mia had never seen Ben get upset before and thought the robed man wouldn't take kindly to getting socked in the face, because that's what it looked like Ben was working up to.

"Well, you might not have, but what of your friend there?" The man sneered at her with even more intensity in his gaze. She got the idea that the man knew what she had done and despised her before he even learned their story. They wouldn't be able to talk their way out of trouble, she could see. "She might think that we would passively allow her to enter the Royal Halls and walk out with whatever *priceless* item that she wanted. She is no princess. She will not ever set foot inside a Royal House again," the robed man seemed to puff up with rage, having obviously gotten to say what he wanted to so badly.

Mia had heard enough and was tired of it. She stepped forward and spoke directly to the robed man who was still staring at her as if she were offending him by simply standing there. "We didn't know that it was the Royal House, okay? It was an accident. I didn't mean to open it, and I don't even know *how* I did it. I thought it was just a wall with some sort of weird design on it. Who are you anyway, to say that we can't leave? We're being peaceful, and we haven't taken a thing."

The robed man raised an eyebrow at her, seeming triumphant about something. "I am the Magistrate of Tancredo. I assume that you are an outsider of Iceworld then, to not know that the robes mark someone of high importance and to think that the Royal Chambers are something as simple as a wall. What is your business in Iceworld? And why should we let you leave if we aren't sure that you aren't a threat?"

Mia shifted uncomfortably, not sure how to answer the second question. "We're going to go see the king so that I can get sent back home. I have no desire to be here or to steal anything while I am in this place."

The magistrate nodded slowly, seeming to contemplate her input. "Hmmm. Well, that changes things." He turned to the waiting villagers and flung his arms into the air, stretching toward the heavens. "The Maze!" he yelled zealously. The villagers all cheered and swarmed closer to the two travelers, grabbing them and pulling them along. One of them took the supplies from Ben's hands and squeezed back through the crowd to return them to the stands they came from.

Mia looked angrily up at the magistrate who was disappearing quickly from view because the villagers were so tightly packed. "I thought you said things had changed!" she yelled after him angrily.

He grinned at her with his evil smirk. "Things *have* changed, but I didn't say that they were *better*, not for *you* at least." He led the way out of the city and toward an enormous wall that was so big that there was nothing else in sight, and the front wall of the labyrinth stretched on and on, never ending.

The villagers kept pushing them along and shoved them toward the only gap. The wall itself was at least twenty-five feet tall, and as they got closer, they saw that the inside of the walls were very thick. Soon the mob behind Ben and Mia shoved the two of them into the maze through the large gap and backed away.

Mia was waiting for something final, something big. When nothing happened, she turned around to taunt, "That's it?" at the villagers, but was cut off. A large wall of ice was moving up as they stood there, filling in the gap so that they could not escape the icy walls that surrounded them. Mia then saw the Magistrate of Tancredo standing on the other side of this wall with a smug look on his face through the ice. "You can't do this!" she yelled through the ice as loudly as she could.

The magistrate simply stood there and smiled. He called softly through the wall, his voice sounding distorted because of the barrier, "Oh, you will find that I can do this. I can do almost anything I want, here in Tancredo." With that, he twiddled his fingers at them and, closely followed by the villagers, turned on his heels and left the two of them stranded in the maze.

Chapter 4: Wizards and Kings

"Let me in," the woman ordered the guard. "The king has asked for me to join him in the workroom." She didn't stand quite as tall as the guard but held the power of authority over him. At least, she should have held that over him.

"The king said that no one is to get in, Wizard. He would've said if I was supposed to let you in." He stood before Wizard Wiesemann and waited for her response with a cocky grin that she longed to permanently remove from his face.

Flustered, she stood a little straighter. "Well, the king sent for me specifically, and here I am. Do you want me to tell him that the boneheaded guard wouldn't let me in, or should I spare you and just turn you into a frog?" she asked quickly and angrily, her head tilted to the side, thinking of the frog charm.

Before the guard could answer, a deep, oily voice came booming through the thick, icy door. "Wiesemann! Get in here, now!" The guard reluctantly opened the door and let Wizard through. She passed through the door, making a face at the guard as she passed.

A pale blonde-haired man had his hands on a worktable, leaning on them heavily. "Wiesemann, how was your argument with the guard today? Really, you should give up any hope that he will pay you any respect. You're all bark and no bite; in fact, you hardly dare to show your teeth. You will never amount to anything more than what you are now, a pathetic magician. I only keep you around because you were already here when I... came into power," he said eloquently.

Wizard seethed inside. She had wished many times that this madman of a king had let her go. She could've at least gotten work from some decent man in a town. *Came into power, you mean that you...* Cutting off the thought, she bowed again. "Yes, Sire. You have been most gracious toward me. I'll never forget what you've done." *That's right; I'll never forget it. The years with you have been the worst seventeen of my life.* "What did you wish to speak to me about, Your Majesty?" she continued, trying to veer him away from her obvious flaws.

"Only wondering a trifle whether or not you've found her yet," he said carefully, slowly, smoothly, and yet venomously. He inspected his sleeve, picking off a piece of dust with his pale, long fingers, seeming supremely disinterested in her.

Wizard gulped. She hoped that the king wouldn't be mad. He had a nasty habit of hiding his anger until the last moment and then throwing her in the dungeon unceremoniously.

Taking a deep breath, she shook her head. "No, Sire. No sign of her yet." She paused, then, "Your Majesty, remind me again why we must find her? There's been no sign of her for seventeen years, why would she turn up now?"

The king looked up at her, his gray eyes cold and mocking. He pushed away from the table he'd been leaning on and walked toward her. "I've told you over and over, Wiesemann. Try to wrap your mind around this: I must speak with her about some... history... that her parents and I have. If she doesn't agree to my conditions, I may have to leave. It's such a nice place here; I'd hate to give it up... And you wouldn't want me to leave either, would you, Wiesemann?" He raised a threatening eyebrow at her, stopping in front of her with his hands folded neatly behind his back.

Of course not! Why would I want you to leave, you pompous, overconfident, greedy, self-absorbed, controlling, evil swine! "No of course not, Sire," she replied expressionlessly. Wizard bowed slightly and backed away.

The king smiled, satisfied at least, as he went back to his throne. "Good, Wizard. Run along and practice some real magic for a change, won't you?" He grinned maliciously at her as she backed towards the door. "Oh, and Wiesemann?" he added delicately.

Wizard stopped in her backward retreat, looking back up at him, wanting him to release her. "Yes, Sire?"

"Don't bother to come back without any important news. I tire of hearing, 'No, Sire, no sign of her yet.' It really is just plain annoying, and it reminds me only of how incompetent you are." With a condescending smile, he turned his back on her, a distinct sign of dismissal.

Out of the door, Wizard straightened up and turned to walk away. She heard the guard behind her chuckling and paused. Having had enough of his disrespect, Wizard concentrated and then snapped her fingers without turning around. Walking away, she heard the dull croak and smiled.

The guard standing at the door had acquired flabby, green skin, webbed hands and feet, and most importantly a dull, hoarse croak of a voice. She had only halfway finished a spell, so he was neither human nor a frog. Whatever he was, he watched her go, furious and a little doleful that she was the only one that could reverse the spell she'd done.

Chapter 5: Katie

Ben and Mia had been walking in the maze for hours upon hours and had come across many different designs etched into the wall of the maze itself. They had seen a ship, a dove, a human, and a snake. Mia had taken one look at all of these and walked on. It was her fault they were in there in the first place, and she didn't want to stay any longer than necessary. It had gotten dark twice already, and it looked as if they would have to spend a third night in the ridiculous ice-puzzle. There was no food, and the two of them were getting very hungry. They walked for a while longer before Ben declared that he wouldn't go any farther.

"I'm tired. Let's rest. Aren't you tired?" He was whinier than she had been when they weren't in the maze. It seemed like the two of them had switched personalities in the crisis that they were currently in. Mia had calmed down and thought things out logically.

"Ben, calm down. We'll stop as soon as we reach the next symbol. I promise." Determined to find the way out, and soon, she stared down the narrow alleyway that served as a path in the labyrinth.

After they walked for a while longer, they came upon an etching of a very small person with pointed ears that stood about four inches high. Ben sank down beside it and looked at it carefully. "It's an Ice Elf," he whispered, "Admittedly a very good one that doesn't look as evil as other ones, but an Ice Elf. Maybe the artist had only ever heard a little bit about them." Seeing Mia's confused expression, he moved to the side so that she could see it as well. "They can freeze anything and have special powers." Curious, he pulled off his glove and ran his hands along the lines of the delicate elf.

"Hey," he said aloud. "The lines aren't part of the wall. Mia, you've gotta feel this." He looked up at her wondrously and saw her apprehensive expression. "C'mon, nothing's going to happen this time."

Mia sighed, more than a little anxious. Ben had a point. It wasn't very likely that this wall would collapse or do anything to get them in even more trouble. She pulled off her glove, looked at the carving dubiously, and ran her fingertips along the lines, like Ben had. Mia was amazed that they actually did seem to be a separate piece. It wasn't that she thought Ben hadn't felt it, but she was surprised how they actually did feel. They weren't sticking very far off the wall, and there was no indication of how they were put there. The lines were so small that Mia could barely feel the ridges under her fingers.

As she felt them, the lines wiggled slightly underneath the pads of her fingers. Yanking her hand back, Mia yelped and stared at the lines. They seemed to shift and stretch as she watched. "Oh yeah, Ben, 'Nothing's going to happen.' Right. HA!" she growled at him. She watched as the lines continued to move and then detach from the wall and gain dimensional substance. They formed a real Ice Elf, not just an engraved picture of one. It shook itself off and looked up at them.

"Hello! I'm Katie," it said. "Thanks for getting me out. It's really crowded in there, too many people and things. Not good at all." The little Elf shook her head, white curls bouncing as she did so. Shrugging her miniscule shoulders, she smiled up at them brightly. "This way!" she commanded cheerfully as she walked down one of the paths.

"Hold on!" Ben called after her frantically. He pulled his glove back on and scrambled to stand up. "Where are you trying to lead us?" He asked suspiciously, looking behind the little Ice Elf as she stopped, a befuddled expression clouding her face.

"What do you mean? Don't you want to get out of here? I sure do. I hate it in here," Katie talked fast, shivering for emphasis as she looked between the two travelers, confused. Panic seemed to line her voice, desperate to do something more exciting than being trapped inside of a wall.

Mia chimed in, "Of course we do, but we've been walking for almost two whole days. Could you give us a few minutes to rest? We're stuck in here and have been trying to find our way out."

Katie relaxed and calmed down. "Oh, okay. You can rest. I like being able to move around anyway. What did you get thrown in for?" The chipper little Elf flopped down and sat cross-legged, watching the humans expectantly.

Mia turned bright red and looked down at Ben, who

had already sunk down and was resting his head against the wall. He shrugged and gestured to the little Elf, still not trusting that she wasn't about to run off with something. "Um, I opened a wall." She looked at Katie sheepishly, unsure how to explain what she'd done any better.

Katie laughed; it was a surprisingly loud and high trill coming from such a small little character. "A wall? How'd you manage that? I thought you could only open doors! Why did you get thrown in for opening a wall? It seems like it'd be a pretty harmless thing to do."

Mia laughed, a little relieved that the Elf wasn't making fun of her, but of the idea. It did sound like a rather odd thing to be able to do. "Well, usually it's only doors, but that particular wall was a door; I just didn't know it. They thought we were trying to steal something from the Royal House." She rolled her eyes before she saw the serious look on the other two's faces. "What?" She suddenly felt sheepish, as if she'd said something she shouldn't have.

Ben looked at her, eyes wide, forcing himself to remember that she wasn't from Iceworld and that she didn't know anything about it; how could she know about this? "Mia, entering a Royal House without the consent of the Royal family is bad. It's like trespassing, only about ten times worse because of whose property it is. We were lucky that they were nice. If it had been any other small village with that kind of importance, you probably would have been forced into a cage for several days, and people would be allowed to pass by and mock you. It would be spread all over Iceworld that we trespassed." He thought a moment and then added, "It probably will be anyway, but nobody knows who we are at least."

Katie nodded solemnly and earnestly. "Yeah, he's right. It's bad." Then she cheered up. "Well, are you two

Iceworld

ready to get going again?" She bounced to her feet and stood up to her full four and a half inches to watch them eagerly.

Mia stood up, nodding dazedly, still thinking over what Ben had said about being thrown into the equivalent of the stocks. "Yeah, I'm ready. Ben, how about you?" She looked down at the boy sitting on the ground beside her.

Ben reluctantly stood up, too. "Yeah, I'm ready. Let's go." He started determinedly off down a path away from them until Katie started to laugh. He paused and turned on his heel to face them, feeling like he had missed some crucial element of the joke. "What?"

Katie managed to slow her giggling enough to say, "Well, do you know where you're going?" Ben shrugged. "The way out is that way." She pointed in the direction opposite Ben, bursting into another fit of giggles.

Ben turned a deep shade of red and his lips pressed together in embarrassment. "Oh. Right, well, Katie, you should probably lead." This time he allowed Katie to go ahead of him. "I won't get in your way this time," he promised, grinning slightly before walking after the Ice Elf, who accepted the leadership and started down the path opposite of the one that Ben had been trying to take.

Before an hour had passed, Katie had led them up and down many paths and straight past others before finally rounding a corner and seeing the light of the outside world in front of them again, instead of just above them. The two humans ran for the open, closely followed by Katie, who was excited by the idea of seeing the outside world again.

Katie had successfully gotten them out of the maze. "There you go. Out like I promised." She sighed and turned back to the icy walls of the maze sadly. She hesitated for a long time and looked as if she was going to move, but did nothing. There was nothing that said that she had to go

~41~

back, and she would really rather not. Yet, she had nowhere to go and nothing to do when she got there, so there was nothing left but to return. Being trapped in between continuous walls wasn't very high on her list of ways to spend her time.

Mia saw the depressed look on Katie's face and offered softly, "You can always come with us. You don't have to go back in there." She smiled kindly at the little Elf, feeling a little pity for the small creature.

Katie looked up at Mia's earnest expression and brightened immediately. "Really? I can? Thanks! You don't know how bad it is in there!" She clambered up onto Mia's shoulder. "So, uh, which way was your camp?" She looked around as if expecting it to be five feet in front of them.

Ben smiled enigmatically. "Hold on and it'll be here in a minute." He whistled sharply on a very high note. Mia smiled at him knowingly. The sound didn't seem very loud, but she was beginning to suspect that Nomis had a magical sense that allowed him to hear it from anywhere and respond to it.

Katie's hands went over her ears as the whistle sounded. She pulled them away once it ended and started asking questions as quickly as she could open her mouth. "What do you mean, 'It'll be here in a minute'? Are you a magician? Is that why you can summon up your camp with a whistle? How can it hear you? Does-" she was cut off by the rush of wings beating the air around them, and she gazed up at the Ice-Dragon in awe.

Nomis landed heavily before them, with all of their equipment still tied on, exactly how they had left him. "Come on, let's get going," Ben said as his stomach grumbled at him. "We still have to get food from the next town, and quickly." He climbed onto Nomis's back and waited for Mia, who had to be even more careful than normal because she had Katie on her shoulder.

"Hang on, Katie," Mia suggested quickly. "The first takeoff is a little unbalancing," she told the Ice Elf on her shoulder.

Katie waved a casual hand at the air, dismissing the comment as if she had ridden on hundreds of dragons before and knew exactly what to expect from this ride. "Okay, let's go." When Nomis took off, she tumbled right off Mia's shoulder and into her hood, where she stayed for the rest of the trip. "Whoa, unbalancing is one thing! How come you didn't tell me I would fall off?"

Mia laughed, "Well, I guess I didn't think about how light-weight you are."

"Humph," was the only response from the small, disgruntled passenger. Katie stayed bunched up in Mia's hood, hanging on, until they stopped less than a mile away from the nearest town.

They had landed on a hill that sloped upward and stopped and then leveled slightly for a sort of ledge. The spot was surrounded by a copse, making a perfect hiding place for the large dragon and his passengers.

Ben jumped off first. "I'll go into the city, alone, this time. Mia, why don't you and Katie stay here? Try not to cause any trouble." He gave her a pointed look and then strode off down the hill toward another city as quickly as he could without tripping over his own feet.

"Huh, fine, Ben! I'll stay here!" Mia grumbled, crossing her arms and glaring after him. "I think that was pretty rude."

Katie laughed at the face Mia was making. "Well, you can't really blame him. It's your fault you ended up in the maze," she pointed out bluntly. This earned her an evil look from Mia, which only made her laugh harder.

"I know, but now we have nothing to do while he's gone." She plopped down on the snow covered ground. Sighing, she rested her chin in her hand. For a while Mia and Katie sat there, and then an idea struck Mia. She flopped onto her back with a *whoosh* of air and started waving her arms and legs in the snow.

Watching Mia carefully, Katie wrinkled her nose and asked, "What are you *doing*? Aren't you cold doing that? I thought humans had higher body temperatures that shouldn't change." She got up and stood over Mia, who was surrounded by a wide imprint in the snow.

"Snow angels!" Mia laughed ecstatically back at her. Standing up carefully, so she wouldn't muss the delicate figure, Mia turned around and watched as the imprint pulled itself off the ground and flew around the clearing like a beautiful specter. The snow angel was made of thousands of individual snowflakes, seemingly unable to join and form an entire figure. She made several more of the stunning creatures and watched them all get up and fly around.

She taught Katie how to make them, but none of the Elf's flew away like hers did. Mia made dozens and every single one of them circled silently around them, staying in the clearing.

*   *   *   *

When Ben came back to the clearing, carrying food, he saw a massive group of swirly, snowy... *things* flying around and panicked. There were plenty of unsavory beasts and animals wandering around Iceworld, and he hoped that Mia hadn't found any. However, she did have a knack for finding trouble, so it wouldn't have surprised him.

Dropping the packages he held, he started searching for the two girls. "Mia? Katie?" Ben searched, ducking and stretching to see as best as he could, for them through the swirling mass. Thinking he caught a glimpse of Mia's coat in the very center, he attempted to brush through one of the swirly objects, and it puffed into a shower of snow all over his face.

Ben, wiping off the dripping remains of the snow, shoved his way through the circle and found Mia and Katie, grabbing Mia's arm. "Are you all right? What happened? What are these things? What did you *do*?" he asked. His face was wet from the melted snow, and she had a hard time keeping a straight face as he stared at her.

Breaking down, Mia smiled and laughed at him. "They're snow angels, Ben. Haven't you ever seen them fly before? And why do you automatically think *I* did it?" Her tone became indignant, and she stopped laughing and watched the snow angels fly away and disappear over the tops of the trees as she lost her will to keep them around.

Ben watched them disappear and then turned again to Mia, slightly annoyed that he'd gotten worked up over her safety for nothing, without even a thank you. "Well, Mia, you're the only one who can open a wall of ice, form a carving into a real elf, and appear from a place that I've never heard of, so I'm going with the gut-instinct that you're the one who did it. And no, I've never seen them fly," he snapped. He wasn't mad, simply disappointed and surprised, but then he never had liked surprises.

Mia's expression hardened. "Fine, it was just a bit of fun while you were gone." She sat down on the snow, starting to feel more than a little upset herself. "Did you get the supplies that we need?"

Ben, wondering when this had turned into a fight, regretted opening his mouth and saying anything. Now Mia was miffed with him, and that was one of the last things that he wanted. Turning red, he replied a little more gently, "Yeah, I've got it all back now. I'll make lunch." He started moving around contemplatively, making a healthy portion of the food into two sandwiches to assuage their starving stomachs, and then he stored the rest carefully away so that no *other* hungry animal would run away with it. Katie didn't need a whole sandwich because of her small size, so she ate the corner of Mia's.

Ben finally cleared his throat and began his apology. "Sorry that I snapped at you, but I really don't like surprises, and it *really* surprised me to see snow angels flying around, and so many of them." He avoided looking at her, adding silently that he didn't like making a fool of himself much either. For a long time, Mia was silent. When Ben looked up anxiously to see whether she was going to accept his apology, she was chewing her food thoughtfully, staring at him as though considering it.

When she had swallowed, Mia replied evenly and a little cryptically, "Well, it's okay about snapping at me, but I think you'll have to get used to surprises."

Ben looked at her quizzically, not understanding what she was getting at. "Why?"

Mia looked at her sandwich, lips pursed, as if it was going to give her the answer to Ben's question, and shrugged. "I don't really know, but I just get this feeling that we're going to get our share of surprises by the time we actually get to Snowsdale." She took another bite thoughtfully.

Ben nodded and sank into his own little trance, reflecting on what she could have meant by that. Mia's words hung in the air as they finished their lunches in silence.

Chapter 6: News

Wizard Wiesemann had been summoned to the Royal Study; the king was perfecting his magic. As she drew closer, she laughed as the guard standing there turned his green flabby face towards her. He croaked, but she couldn't tell what he said.

"Sorry, what? You really shouldn't croak. No one can understand a word you say." She was being a tad contemptuous, but held no remorse. The guard had given her too much grief over the years. Wizard pushed through the door into the workroom. Usually she didn't have anything new to say, but today she did. She entered the room tentatively, for the king could be very easy to anger.

"Wiesemann, I thought I told you not to come back without news of her," thundered the king's oily, deep voice from within the room. Wizard couldn't see the speaker, but she concluded that he must be invisible somewhere within the same four walls or she wouldn't be able to hear him at all. She wasn't sure if it made her more or less anxious about speaking to him.

"Y-yes, Sire. I *have* brought news of the girl," Wizard said the best she could to the room. The king suddenly materialized before her, standing too close, with nostrils flaring, and eyes wide and terrifying.

"You are sure, Wiesemann? Sure that it's not some unfortunate girl that you have mistaken her for?" he asked in a strained voice, as if the wrong answer would earn her a nice punishment. Wizard knew that it was exactly the case.

"I'm p-positive, Sire. It could be no one else," Wizard said as she took a hasty step away from the menacing king. "While I was searching the kingdom's reports, like you ordered, I heard that she has been in a city south of here, approximately halfway across Iceworld. She seems to be on her way here." She waited nervously as the king thought over her words, leaning away from her and giving her some breathing room.

"Show me," he barked the order at her. He pulled a scroll from the shelf and unfurled it to reveal a map of the entirety of Iceworld and stood impatiently waiting for Wiesemann to point to a city.

Wizard jumped forward quickly and pointed a shaky finger at the city that she meant. She thought it over for a moment and then nodded, reassured that she was right.

The king stared at it hungrily and then snapped his head around to face her. "Tell the Captain of the Guard to send a small, elite team down there to investigate. Do you think you can manage that simple task, Wiesemann?" With a malicious grin turning up the corners of his mouth, he turned back to look back at the map. "Soon," he assured himself. "Very soon indeed."

Wizard sighed and bowed again, leaving the room quickly. "Yes, Sire. As you wish." Walking at a brisk and steady pace, Wizard grumbled to herself, irate. *'Do you think you could do that, Wiesemann?' I can do a lot more than* you *seem to think! What a pompous idiot!* Before she could continue ranting inside her head, however, she realized that she had come to the door of the Captain of the Guard, who oversaw all military and defenses of the kingdom or, since the king took over, the defense of the king and the offense of the kingdom.

Wizard knocked three times and waited patiently as the captain came to the door. "Yes, Wizard Wiesemann? What is it?" He, unlike many of his guards, showed her due respect and didn't call her Wiesemann, which was an insult to her authority by subordinates. Those who called her Wizard were friends and used her title as a nickname.

Wizard sighed and reluctantly began to inform the captain. "I believe we've found her. The king wants you to send a small, highly skilled group of men to a city south of here. Recently, there was a girl who matched the description of the one we've been looking for. We have to find out where she was going." The captain gestured her inside the room, inviting her in. She strode into the office and examined the map.

The captain scratched his head, following her over to the map and inspected it himself. "Well, all of my trained men are highly skilled, but I think I can manage to find a few suitable for a road trip. Where am I sending them, may I ask?"

Wizard nodded slowly and pointed at a city in the center of the map. "Here, Captain. This is where she is supposed to have been seen." She turned to look at him solemnly.

The captain turned to look at her, shocked and a little incredulous. "Tancredo?" he asked, checking to see that it was the city that she had meant. "But nothing has happened there in years."

Wizard simply shrugged and replied, "Yes. Tancredo."

Chapter 7: Magic

"I still don't know how you do that," Katie whined. "I can't, and neither can Ben."

Mia had demonstrated how she had made the snow angels, but when the others tried, hers were the only ones that ever flew away. "To tell you the truth, I don't really know all that well myself," she replied, a little amazed by this herself. Mia had never been special at anything, and now that she was, it was a strange experience to her. "It must be the same thing that happened with the gate in Tancredo and with Katie in the maze." There was no logical explanation that she could think of for the things that had happened. Then again, she couldn't think of a logical explanation for Iceworld, Frost Dragons, and Ice Elves either, so perhaps it was better if she didn't try to find one.

Ben walked into the camp and said simply, "I think it was magic." When Mia and Katie turned to stare at him, he explained further. "As far as I know, only a few people besides Mia can do that kind of thing or anything like it. So, I figure it must be magic."

Katie stood up, shaking her head impetuously. "No, watch this. *This* is magic." She raised her arms and concentrated. Before long Ben and Mia could see that she was creating an icy blob mid-air. Then the blob began to take on a shape. It twisted and arched and wrinkled until it looked like skin and scales. Slowly it evolved into an ice sculpture of Ben and Mia riding Nomis, but something wasn't normal.

The ice Mia was in front of Ben and was reclined gently against his chest, her head leaning back slightly. The ice Ben's cheek was resting on her hair. She appeared to be sleeping and he gently held her in place as Nomis flew silently, caught in place by Katie's image.

"Stop," said both humans, turning deep red. Ben swept the sculpture out of the air and buried it with snow with his foot before it could form any expressions; he didn't want to know what kind of emotions Katie's imagination could whip up.

"Uh...we'd better get going," he said awkwardly and a little gruffly, trudging the deep snow to their belongings. He grabbed the packs and tossed them on to Nomis, tying them in place.

Katie giggled and looked surreptitiously up at Mia, who had also turned red. The Ice Elf laughed louder until she climbed into Mia's hood for take-off. Nomis spread his wings and had just started to flap them in the air when Mia shrieked.

She vaulted clumsily off the dragon's back, hit the ground, and stumbled, falling abruptly to her knees. Mia barely paused for a moment before she picked herself up only to drop to her knees again in the exact spot she had been sitting moments before. Digging desperately through the snow, Mia started to sob heavily, gasping for air.

Ben hurriedly stopped Nomis from taking off without Mia. He hopped off and ran over to her. Not knowing what to do to comfort a crying girl, Ben felt at a loss. Stooping beside her, he asked gently, "What did you lose?" He felt silly questioning her, but he felt that maybe if he knew, then he could help look for it.

Mia just sat catatonically, having given up. "It's not here. I can't believe I lost it." Tears still rolled down her cheeks steadily.

Ben tried not to sound as panicked as he was feeling. "Can't believe you lost what?" Fortunately, he was better at concealing emotions in his voice than Mia was.

Sniffling, Mia answered quietly, "My mother's necklace. It's all I have left of her, and it's gone."

Knowing the answer already, Ben asked, just as quietly, "All you have left? What do you mean?" He watched as Mia kneeled in the churned up snow, crying.

"She died ten years ago, when I was seven. Dad got rid of all of her things because he couldn't bear to think of her, I think. That necklace was the only thing that I have left of her because she gave it to me before she died. It was a small, delicate snowflake. And now, it's... gone."

She put her face in her hands and cried. Ben, more awkward now than ever, knelt beside her and patted her on the shoulder. "I'll help find it."

"Me, too!" Katie started digging around in the snow enthusiastically, willing to help her new friends with anything.

Mia clenched her teeth, suddenly furious at herself. "It's not fair!" she screamed, pounding her balled up fists on her legs. A slight wind picked up, shifting the snow around them in circles and even blew the little Ice Elf off her feet. "Hey! What's going on?" She ran over to Ben and crawled up onto his shoulder, hanging on to the seam of his jacket. "Take cover!"

The wind was getting stronger and stronger until Ben was driven to take shelter among the trees. Mia was the only one who didn't seem bothered by the wind at all. She sat in the same spot, seething and furious.

Suddenly, in a movement so quick that Ben suspected he would have missed it if he had blinked, all the snow was shoved out of the clearing, leaving the perfectly level ground bare and frost-covered underneath.

Standing up, Mia didn't see it but swayed gently, as if she were very tired. Not far from where Mia was standing, a small, silver snowflake lifted itself from the snow. There was a bright, thin silver chain hanging from the delicate snowflake. It was the necklace that she had lost.

Slowly, the necklace flew toward Mia, as if suspended in the air by an invisible thread. It hovered before her as she wiped tears from her eyes and looked up. Spotting the dangling necklace in front of her, Mia stared at it and gently took it in her hand. As soon as her gloved hand touched the metal the wind that Mia couldn't feel faded away.

Ben and Katie saw all this from their hiding spot. They came out quickly, now that the wind had died away. Ben simply shook his head and said, "Magic." He looked over at Mia as she turned around. Suddenly she looked very tired and shakily attempted to walk over to Nomis.

When she had covered half the distance, her legs gave out and she started to fall to the ground. Ben, seeing this as it happened, dashed forward and just managed to catch her

Iceworld

before her head bounced off the frigid ground.

    Gasping, Mia shook herself awake and tried to push herself back onto her feet, brushing Ben's arms away from her waist carefully. "Come on, let's go," she mumbled, barely coherent. She waited as he walked skeptically past her and got on Nomis. As he passed, Katie jumped onto Mia's coat.

    "That wasn't magic! That was sorcery! Mia, you're a sorceress! How did you do that? That's the necklace you lost, isn't it? I'll bet it is." She sounded very excited by the prospect and stared wide-eyed at the human girl as if expecting some other sort of magical demonstration.

    Mia hated to dampen her spirits, but she felt she didn't have a choice, especially given how tired she suddenly felt. "No, I'm not a sorceress. I don't know how I did it, and yes, it is my necklace," she replied shortly. Yawning widely, she climbed onto Nomis behind Ben. She sat down, rested her head on Ben's back, and waited patiently as the dragon took off, carefully holding her necklace tight in her hand.

    Ben looked over his shoulder at her once, but she gave him a dark look that indicated for him not to say anything in front of Katie. Mia had no desire for another list of questions that she could barely answer. He nodded understandingly and faced forward again.

    They flew on for several hours before finally coming upon a point where they could settle down for the night. When they got off Nomis, Ben turned to Katie immediately. "Hey, Katie, could you find us a place where we could set up our stuff?"

    Katie beamed. "Sure! No problem!" She ran off to find a suitable spot.

    Ben looked back at Mia seriously. "So, any idea what happened back there?" He was feeling a little impatient, but he knew that he couldn't force an answer out of Mia if she didn't want to give it.

Mia glared at him and avoided the question by asking, "Won't Katie hear us?" She turned away from him, making sure her necklace was on securely, laying her fingers on it gently.

"No," he answered bluntly. "Now answer the question, Mia. Don't change the subject." Ben took her by the shoulders and turned her around, looking deeply into her crystal blue eyes. "C'mon, Mia, tell me what happened. You can trust me."

Mia shook her head, looking away. "If I could tell you, I would, Ben, but I don't know what it was. Maybe Katie is right. Maybe it is sorcery. I have absolutely no idea. I was so upset about losing Mom's necklace." A small tear escaped from the corner of her eye. "I don't plan for these things to happen, Ben. They just do."

Ben, feeling that he'd bitten off more than he could chew, let go of her and stepped away to get their things. "I believe you, Mia, I do, but you have to try to get it under control. What if something really bad happens? I can't do magic or sorcery or whatever that was to help us or reverse whatever you may do." He turned again to look at Mia's face. He saw the tear clinging to her cheek and came closer, gently wiping it off. "And don't cry. It's weird for me because I have no idea what to do," he joked with her.

Mia let out a strangled laugh. "Really? You're doing just fine right now." She smiled lightly up at him. It occurred to both that his hand was still caressing her cheek.

Before either could say anything, Katie, looking excited about something, ran back over the small hill that sheltered them. Suddenly, she stopped and smiled mischievously. "Sorry, am I interrupting?" She laughed as Ben and Mia stepped away from each other, turning red again. Instantly forgetting the way she had just found them, she began to blurt out what she'd found. "You guys will never guess what I just saw! It's a bunch of men in uniforms, and they're coming from the direction we're going. Maybe they can give us directions!"

Ben's face darkened visibly. "Uniforms? They're soldiers." He followed as Katie led the two of them to the spot where she had seen the soldiers.

"There they are," Katie breathed when they got to the place. Peeking over the lip of a snow drift, she looked at the men in matching uniforms that were marching along in perfect lines.

Ben glared at them with loathing from their hiding place. Picking up Katie, he grabbed Mia by the wrist and started leading them back to Nomis. "We're moving as far away as we can from those guys."

"Ben, what's wrong?" Mia asked, pushing at his hand in an attempt to make him to let go.

Ben let go of her and climbed as quickly as he could on to Nomis's back. "Nothing, but those guards are all but comforting. Now c'mon, let's get out of here!" He reached down and tried to pull her up on to Nomis behind him.

Mia dug in her heels. "Ben," she called up to him, "What are you doing?"

"I'm going to make sure that those soldiers don't come near us." He looked at them seriously, as if thinking she was dense for not understanding the concept.

Mia made a face at him. "We're not going anywhere until you tell me what your problem with the soldiers is. We haven't done anything to make them upset with us."

"But they've done something to upset me, Mia," Ben snapped in reply, getting testy now that she wasn't going along with his sudden plan.

"Well, that's obvious," Mia snorted derisively.

Ben dismounted and turned around to face her angrily, his face red, "Look, about thirteen years ago, soldiers came to my house and demanded that we move, because we were too far away to keep under control. When my father refused to obey, they struck him down. He was hit on the head with one of the soldier's weapons. The soldiers left, and Mom brought Dad to lie down on the bed. He stayed there for five days before he died. Dad was just lying there, looking at the ceiling, and he stopped, just stopped living." Ben, shaking from the memory, looked at the ground and then at Nomis, avoiding looking at Mia's face.

"Oh, Ben, I'm so sorry," Mia said sadly, her brow furrowing in sympathy. "I know what it's like to lose a parent. It was so horrible for me when my mom died." She shook her head, looking at the ground and then looked straight up at Ben, who was still avoiding meeting her eye. "I'm not Medusa, you know."

"Sorry," he mumbled, but he didn't quite meet her eye yet. "It happened so long ago, but I can still remember it clearly. I'll never forgive the guards." He finally looked up at her, defiance in his eyes. "They're horrible and cold and spiteful and selfish and—"

Mia nodded and cut him off gently. "I don't expect you to forgive them, Ben. We'll probably have to go past them to meet the king at the castle. So, you'll just try to ignore them when we get there. For now, I think we need to be ready to encounter them soon." She smiled very, very lightly at him.

"Yeah, I understand." Ben turned away. For awhile, Mia watched him sitting erect before she started to move around, unpacking supplied for dinner. "Will you send Nomis away and make dinner?" she asked him over her shoulder.

Ben shrugged and stood. "Why?"

"Because the soldiers are coming."

"I'd really rather not deal with them," Ben said quickly.

"We can ask for directions. We wouldn't have to 'deal with them' for long. Plus, it would be an advantage to actually know we were going in the right direction and how long it'll take us to get there," Mia reasoned with him.

"You can. Go right ahead, but I'm not going to. I am not going to ask any soldier anything." Ben stubbornly folded his arms.

"Fine, I'll go. See you in a few minutes." Mia stepped around him, actually planning on going. She looked at him pointedly and kept walking.

"All right, I'll come with you, but I'm not going to say a thing."

"Fine by me." She waited as he got the water simmering and told Nomis to retreat into the woods.

Mia walked until she could see the soldiers and waved to get their attention. The man that appeared to be the captain nodded to her and dispatched two of the men he was leading to go and talk to her before walking on with the others.

When they got close enough, the soldiers regarded the two of them carefully until Mia spoke. "We seem to be lost. Could you tell us how to get to Snowsdale from here?" Mia asked politely. She wished Ben would stop glaring murderously at the two men; it was less than helpful.

The younger of the two soldiers nodded and agreed to follow them back to the camp. He explained in detail where Snowsdale was and how to get there, gesturing somewhat wildly in the air.

While Mia was getting directions, Ben and the second soldier were eyeing each other with distaste. Ben forced himself to keep the accusatory glare out of his look while serving the stew. The soldier made no effort to hide his dislike of common folk. He found them a waste of time. Their opinion didn't matter; it was the king's that did.

Once she had learned where Snowsdale was, Mia thanked the soldier kindly, let them finish their meal, saw them on their way, and then turned to Ben with a smug expression. "See, that wasn't so bad, was it?"

Ben grumbled instead of answering. He looked over his shoulder as the soldiers drifted off in another direction. When Nomis returned, they swiftly unrolled sleeping bags and climbed into them for a good-night's sleep. They would soon be flying off in the direction of Snowsdale.

* * * *

"Sir, I don't know what it was, but it was *big*. I think we should try to find out what it was so that we know what kind of monster they're harboring!" The older of the two soldiers Ben and Mia had met was telling his commanding officer. "The footprints were absolutely enormous; they didn't even think of trying to cover them up.

The officer rubbed the sides of his head, shaking it from side to side. "You forget that we're on a mission for King Dimitri. We have no use of gallivanting off after some creature that isn't doing us any harm as of right now. You're not to search for whatever the beast was," he ordered firmly. He sighed and sat down near the fire that the men had started. He didn't particularly care about what made the enormous footprints as long as it didn't interfere with his orders.

Chapter 8: In Tancredo

"What do you mean, you don't know?" the soldier officer roared at the robed man who glared back at him with extreme distaste.

"I mean what I say. I don't have a clue as to where in the Maze they are, just that it is nearly impossible for them, or anyone else," he added with a sneer at the soldiers, "to get out. That maze is designed to keep people trapped inside. I am the Town Magistrate, not a psychic," the robed man said, slamming the door in their faces as he finished.

The officer snarled and turned to his men who were standing behind him. "Break it down," he ordered.

The thickest of the guards backed up while the others scrambled out of the way. The man charged the door only to have it smash to the floor easily, with him on top.

The robed man simply stood to the side, giving them an icy glare from inside his home. "I already told you there is no possible way to track people once they go into the Maze. Even if there was, there is no way to reach them. The walls are thirty feet tall and half a foot thick. They are protected and shifted by magic. It would take more force than you can possibly imagine to break through it. I've told you what you want. Now return my door to the way it was." He marched stiffly deeper into his house.

The large guard picked up the door and fitted it neatly back into place, careful not to knock it back over. The frustrated officer took out a small looking glass that Wizard Wiesemann had enchanted for the guards to use so that they could contact the captain back in Snowsdale. "Captain," he said tentatively. A minute later the weary face of the captain swam to the surface of the little mirror.

"Yes, Dawlin?" his voice came faintly. Only a very slight look of hope showed on his weathered face. "Please, tell me that it's good news."

"Sorry, sir. She managed to open the local Royal House, and they threw her into the Tancredo Maze. There doesn't seem to be a way to get her out if she's still in there, and there's no way to tell if she is. However, we did find out that she was traveling north with a young man that is around her own age. Most of the villagers didn't pay attention to how they looked, but almost all of them said that they could tell that the two of them weren't related. The magistrate said that she had black hair, blue eyes, and was hot-tempered. The young man had brown hair and brown eyes and was slightly taller than she. Neither of them said their names though," he said quickly.

The captain looked worried, "King Dimitri won't be happy about that. I'm glad I'm not Wizard; I don't have to

Iceworld

tell him the bad news. Head back here for now." He faded from the view of his men. Thinking about it for a moment, he decided that there was only one thing to do at that point.

Sighing, he reached his hand out for a small rope and frowned. He didn't understand it, but pulled the rope anyway to summon Wizard. The magic-worker had staged it so that if anyone pulled one of these little ropes, she would know and would be able to come to them as soon as she could. The complexities and possibilities of magic baffled him and made him glad that he went into the military of the kingdom instead.

Before long, Wizard strode into the captain's office. "Yes?" She looked hopeful, but her face fell when she saw his expression. "Oh great, I guess I'll have to go and tell the king…" She felt depressed before the captain said a word.

"They said that she opened the local Royal House in Tancredo," the captain called after her as she started to exit. Wizard paused and stared into the distance, as if hit with a sudden realization.

"Thank you, captain," she replied shortly before disappearing down the corridor.

Going through the halls, Wizard mumbled distractedly to herself. She headed for the Throne Room because the king was usually in there at this time of day.

Once, years ago, the Throne Room had been occupied regularly and was used for listening and responding to subjects' problems. The kings and queens of old would then help in any way that they saw fit. But the current king was not so kind or patient. He refused to let commoners into the palace at all, much less to hear their complaints.

King Dimitri was sitting slumped in his throne, the picture of bad posture. He looked tiredly bored, as if he had nothing better to do than sit there, though he brightened very slightly as Wizard stepped into the room and bowed to him. "Yes, Wizard, what news do you have?"

"I'm a-afraid t-that there is l-little good, Sire," Wizard said shakily, fearing what he would do to her once he knew. "Ah... the soldiers failed to capture her. But they did get a description of her and her traveling companion. She fits the description and has an advanced magical ability, advanced enough to open the Royal House in Tancredo." She waited on edge as the king took in this information.

King Dimitri nodded and looked at her carefully, eyes narrowed. "I expected as much. Even when all you had to do was order other men to go, you still fouled it up. Well, I don't think it would be wise for you to keep making a mess of things. You'll be well served by... taking a little break from your duties." He glared at Wizard who fought the sudden urge to blink, knowing he was using magic on her. The moment she closed her eyes for the briefest second, she saw that she had been transported to the dungeon.

She sighed exasperatedly. King Dimitri had sent her to a magic repellent cell; there was no escape until someone was told to release her. Wizard sat down on the cold, hard floor, resigning herself to a long wait.

The king, meanwhile, sent an order to the Captain of the Guard to watch Slippit Road for any sign of the girl they were looking for and to bring her to the castle immediately.

Chapter 9: The Mountains

Mia sighed. She felt that deep down something was wrong. "Ben, I don't think we should fly over the road anymore."

Ben looked over his shoulder at her with wide eyes. "Are you crazy? Why shouldn't we? This is the fastest way!"

"Please, Ben, I have a really creepy feeling about it. Let's go northwest from here, through the mountains," She suggested, rubbing her arms unconsciously, as if trying to push her goose-bumps back into her skin. Mia, looking in the direction she had indicated, could see the mountains' tall spikes jutting up into the sky. The mountains were dark gray and loomed over them, even from this distance. They we frightening, but she would feel safer surrounded by the lonely stone than out in the open.

Ben intruded on her grim thoughts, confirming them

as well. "You *are* crazy! Mia, those mountains are dangerous. Lots of people have gone in, but only a few very lucky ones *ever* make it back out."

"Then why is there a road leading into the mountains? Couldn't they just follow that?" inquired Mia, having spotted the thin ribbon of ice below them splitting into two paths, one going straight for the mountains and the other into empty land.

Shaking his head unbelievingly, Ben explained, "The road originally went into the mountains, but when more and more people started disappearing, to the fork was created to offer a new route so that it wouldn't happen anymore. Some people still go in." Seeing the look on Mia's face, he quickly added, "And I don't want to be one of them and get stuck in there for the rest of my life!"

"Ben! Come on, you don't really believe that do you? It's probably just a story." Try as he might, Mia refused to fly along the road and argued with him until he agreed, under the condition that they ate before they entered the mountains; that way they could leave more quickly.

Katie grumbled as they entered the mountains. She hated being closed in by solid walls after being trapped between them in the Maze. She had seen enough walls to last her a lifetime.

* * * *

As they passed through, an old lady who had built her home near the mountains sadly watched them pass. She shook her head and went back to her house work. Although she had seen many go into the mountains, none returned, and she hardly expected these kids to be any different.

* * * *

Ben had planned on flying straight through the mountains without stopping. For many hours there were no problems whatsoever, but Nomis became weary from flying for such a long time. His wings went farther and farther down, and with each stroke, they became harder to bring back up. The group started to dip lower and lower as darkness slowly closed in around them.

Soon, it was entirely dark, and Mia could hardly see Ben in front of her. Nomis could barely keep them in the air, even straining himself. All of a sudden, he stopped beating the air with his wings. They began a wild freefall through the darkness.

Completely helpless, Mia leaned back from the sheer force of the drop, a scream tearing from her throat. Katie had crawled into the pack and hid there, her arms curled over her head protectively, and even Ben was yelling. At the last minute, Nomis seemed to come around again and just managed to spread his wings, catching the air violently.

They crashed heavily and skidded through the dirt. The riders fell off and landed on the ground, groaning. The landing had been anything but graceful. Ben was sprawled face up on the ground, face twisted in agony, his wrist beneath him. Mia wasn't far away, sprawled face down with her arms curled around her. When the ground stopped shaking and dirt stopped raining from the sky, she looked up and glanced around.

The ground at the base of the mountains was covered in sparse, scraggly brushes and bunches of grass. Small rocks littered the entire area, giving everything a rather gray, bleak look. It wasn't long before Mia became aware of groaning coming from nearby.

"Ben, are you okay?" she asked, her voice high. She rolled over and sat up, holding a scraped knee and elbow.

"I think I broke something." He sat up slowly. Gently handling the wrist he landed on, Ben winced. "Ouch!"

Standing up, he started kicking the loose rocks around in a truly irate way. "Great! We're stuck in the mountains overnight, my wrist is broken, and Nomis is asleep! He's only ever been this tired once before, and that time I couldn't get him up for over a day!" Storming over to Mia, he extended his good hand and pulled her to her feet.

"That's... bad," Mia said hesitantly, not sure how to respond to his rant. Settling upon something she might be able to help with, she focused on his wrist and reached for it.

"Don't touch it," he warned, jerking his entire arm out of her reach. "It already hurts."

"I just want to see how bad it is, you big baby," said Mia, rolling her eyes but keeping her attention on his wrist. She pulled off his glove and was amazed at how swollen it was already. The entire wrist was red and puffy with some definite signs of incredible bruising. Mia laid her cold finger-pads very lightly against the swelling. Ben pulled his arm away again, but winced from the sudden pain caused by the jerk. "Yep, that's broken," she confirmed, looking carefully at the red, purple, and black wrist.

Ben groaned from frustration and pain. "Perfect. We don't have the supplies we need to make a splint either..." He kicked the ground, succeeding only in making another scuff mark on the ground.

Mia wrinkled her brow and thought hard. "Let me see your wrist again," she said delicately, reached for it again, even more gently than before. When Ben tentatively held out his hand, she took it and closed her eyes. Concentrating all she could on healing the broken bones inside his wrist, Mia pictured his wound knitting itself well again. In her hands, the heat of Ben's swollenness went down and his wrist returned to normal. When she opened her eyes, she was holding on to his perfectly healed wrist.

Testing his joint, Ben was amazed at what Mia had done. "Wow, you got the magic to come when you wanted it that time..." He stared at Mia as she pulled back from him, suddenly irritable.

"I just concentrated on it. Now can we *please* sort out our stuff?" she asked agitatedly as she bent down and grabbed a bag roughly. Stalking around, Mia picked up what they needed for dinner and started setting up.

Ben pulled his glove on again and came over to help get the fire started. "Why don't you just, uh, cool off for a bit, and I'll make dinner," he suggested. Mia nodded and walked around, gathering the rest of their equipment.

As she circled Nomis, she saw a package had been thrown into shadows at the base of the mountains. Sighing heavily, Mia reached out a hand to grab it. It was her surprise when another hand reached out and snatched hers, yanking her sharply away from the dragon. She shrieked from fear and shock before she was completely immersed in dark shadows and her captor's other strong hand was laid tightly over her mouth.

Ben came running. "Mia? Are you okay?" He looked around without finding her and then uneasily returned to the fire, apparently thinking she had gone for a walk and would return soon.

A rough whisper in her ear came from the person holding her. "Don't struggle. I need to speak with you..." He pulled her towards the mountain and into what seemed to be a twisting and dark tunnel.

Mia didn't fight. She felt the strength in the calloused hands and knew that they could easily wring her neck if they so wished. Stumbling along backwards down endless tunnels, Mia followed her captor, having no other choice available to her. Even if she had been thinking clearly, Mia couldn't have gotten back out, the tunnels were so convoluted.

Finally, her captor cast her to the ground. When he turned to look at her, she saw the dark hair, and bright, bright blue eyes in the light of a fire. "What do you want?" she asked fearfully, pulling away from him.

The man turned to look at her, shock emanating from his face. He was younger than Mia had expected, his face unlined, though his hair was streaked with grey. His eyes were bright blue, in the most familiar way. Shaking off the feeling that she should know the man, Mia turned her attention back to what he was saying.

"Please, don't be afraid. I simply want you to help me." His voice was deep but raspy, as if he hadn't used it for a while. "Your friend seemed a little quick to judge, and you would have fought or screamed if I had tried the more traditional method. Besides, I don't want that dragon after me if I can help it."

Mia sat up a little straighter. "How can I help you?" She didn't know anything about this strange man. He wore tattered and patched clothing. Holes were patched with animal fur and were, in some places, already wearing thin. Perhaps he had once lived in a town and had come to the mountains, without leaving, long ago.

"There are so many travelers wandering around, lost in these stone monsters. They come in here trying to find a short cut, but the new road was built for a reason: so that people could go around these mountains. You can help me get the travelers out of the mountains." He shook his head and sat down across from her, looking weary.

Sighing, he continued, rubbing his temples, "My name is Trin." He looked up at Mia carefully. "I live here, and every day I come across some random traveler stumbling around." He chuckled grimly. "Don't get me wrong. I like company, but I don't want it when all there is are strangers that want nothing more than to get out of this Godforsaken place."

Mia watched him cautiously, sizing him up, deciding how much of a threat he truly was to her. He was probably a few years younger than her father. He didn't seem to pose any immediate threat. "What do you want me to do?" she asked hesitantly.

Trin looked up as if he had forgotten that she was there. "We'd need a large beacon to summon the travelers to one location so that we can lead them out of the mountains and they can go home to their families and friends. That's where you'll come in. I saw the magic you did on the boy's arm. Do you think you could do this as well?" He sounded confident, but was being polite.

"I don't know," Mia responded, unsure. "That's the first time it happened when I planned it. I don't know if I could do it again." She hugged her knees to her chest, though she was no longer afraid of him.

Trin nodded thoughtfully and looked at the fire. "You just need to focus. We'll have to be careful how we do it though... We don't want you overexerting yourself." He looked up at her again. "I can help a little. I have never been able to do magic, but I knew someone who could."

He stood and paced a bit. "It won't be difficult, but we'll have to know when to stop." Trin helped Mia to her feet. "I'll take you back to your camp. Your friend will be worried. Perhaps it would be better if you spoke to him before he sees me in person."

Mia nodded slowly in agreement. "Yeah. Probably. I'll help you, but like I said, I don't know the first thing about this."

Trin smiled and bowed. "Of course. I'll lead you back out of the cave and wait by the entrance while you talk to your friend."

So, Mia followed Trin back up the tunnels without realizing the path they were taking. When they reached the exit, he nodded, encouraging her, and she went out alone to face Ben.

Ben was sitting in front of their fire, poking at his dinner, his face anxious, when Mia re-entered the camp. He jumped up and set the meal down, running over to her.

"Mia, where have you been? What's wrong?" he asked as he saw the odd look sketched across her face and put a hand on her arm. "Are you okay, Mia?"

"Nothing, Ben. I'm fine." Shaking her head, Mia brushed past him, sat down, and gestured for him to do the same. Knowing that she should be direct, Mia took a deep breath and began, "Ben, there's a man who lives in the mountains. I've been talking with him. He says that there are a lot of lost travelers wandering around with no idea where to go. He wants my help getting them out of here, and he's going to show me what to do. I agreed to help." She looked at him across the fire, trying to gauge his reaction.

Ben laughed, relieved that her temper had improved after a walk around. "Okay, funny joke, Mia. Now really, where'd you go?" He looked at her trying to straighten his face, but laughter kept folding it back up.

Mia's jaw dropped. "You think I'm joking?"

Ben surrendered and allowed himself to laugh again. "Well, yeah. Really, who in Iceworld are you going to meet in these mountains that knows how to do magic? Magic is rare enough without adding stupidity to it for coming in here."

Trin stepped out from behind Nomis. "Me, and I don't strictly know magic." He looked at Ben disapprovingly. "You shouldn't be so quick to disregard what your companion says, Ben. By the way, neither Mia nor I are stupid." He sat down beside Mia as he spoke.

Ben scrambled backward from the shock, falling onto his butt in his haste. Mia had been telling the truth and not some massive story after all. "O-okay…" was all Ben could say for a moment, but once Trin sat down, Ben had questions. "Where the heck did you come from? Why are you in the mountains? Who are you?"

"I came from Snowsdale, and I chose to come here. My name is Trin," the tattered man replied, answering all of Ben's questions. "I need Mia's assistance to get all these travelers out of my home. We had hoped that you would support this plan."

Mia looked back and forth between the two men as Trin stared at Ben, whose eyes were distrusting and suspicious. "I'm going to help him, Ben. He knows the way around the mountains. If anyone can get us out, Trin can," she told him, putting complete confidence in her new acquaintance. She wasn't sure why she did this, but it seemed right, like it fit. There was something about Trin that was comforting and reminiscent of her family.

Ben's gaze flickered in her direction and then back to Trin, and he gave in. "Fine, but if anything goes wrong…"

"I know. My responsibility," Trin said, as if finishing Ben's thought. "I'll come and speak to you in the morning. Good night." He stood up and left them at their fire.

Ben watched him go. When Trin was out of earshot and eyesight, he turned to Mia accusingly and asked, "You trust just about anyone, don't you?"

Mia narrowed her eyes in response to the question.

"You won't trust anyone, will you?"

"No. And for good reason."

"Not everyone is out to get us, Ben."

Ben glared. "Fine, tell me about where you're from then," he growled, desperate for something to calm him down.

Mia, startled, shook her head, her silky hair swaying back and forth, catching the light. "Why? There's nothing interesting about it."

Gifted as he was in reading Mia's emotions, Ben looked up at her, perplexed. She was avoiding looking at him and was picking at a piece of lint from her coat. "Mia? What happened back there?"

"Nothing, Ben."

"Then tell me. I want to know more about you. Has it occurred to you that all we really know about each other is that each of us has had a parent die? It's ridiculous that we know almost nothing about each other and have traveled this far."

Gaping, the corners of Mia's lips twitched. "I guess it is. All right. My world has four seasons. Spring, summer, autumn, and winter. Spring is when all the snow melts…" Mia continued to describe her world to an amazed Ben. Even Katie came out and sat listening in awe.

When she finished her narrative, Ben shook his head in near disbelief. "So," he started with difficulty, "why do you hate talking about it? It seems so great. You get to run around when it's warm, swim in water that isn't freezing, and feel the grass sway against your ankles. Why didn't you want to talk about it?"

Mia, uncomfortable again, looked down and then back up at him. His eyes were full of wonder and innocent curiosity. Taking a deep breath and letting it out slowly,

Mia braced herself for what was about to spill out of her mouth.

"My dad... he's... not right." The words came haltingly, but they came and kept coming. "He was a fun-loving guy. He and Mom would take me to the beach and toss me into the water and play tag with me. He even taught me how to tie my shoes.

"After Mom died... when Mom died ten years ago, something happened to him that I can't explain. He snapped. It's like he barely thinks his life was worth living anymore. Half the time he's not even in his right mind. He started calling me Diane and swearing and throwing things, yelling that I left him alone in this world and that I'll pay for it. That even though I'm dead, he'll make me wish that we'd never come to that place and that he should have just followed the law and let me marry the other man."

A tear dropped onto her hand. Taking a deep, shaking breath, Mia swiped a hand over her eyes. "Then he'll come back to himself and sink down onto the couch holding his head and whimpering. He apologizes for everything that's said and takes his sleeping pills that knock him out and let him rest through the night. He's never the dad I knew when I was growing up."

Ben stared at her as her tears fell faster and faster, until she was sobbing uncontrollably. Then he got up and went to sit by her, wrapping his arms awkwardly around her as he'd seen his mother do. With Mia's head against his chest, he stroked her hair until her sobbing subsided and she was left quietly hiccupping. Releasing her, Ben scooted away from her enough to let her have her space.

"I'm sorry. I never would have brought it up if..." *If I knew what you'd gone through...* he wanted to add, but Mia seemed to sense it anyway. "I can understand why you didn't want to talk about it."

Mia nodded, her eyes blank and hollow. "Yeah. It's easier to think about now though. Thanks, Ben, for letting me unload. I've never told anyone about my dad before." She smiled sheepishly up at her friend. "I'm kinda tired now, though."

"Then let's go to sleep." Ben stood and went to his bedroll, lying down. Soon he was asleep, rolled up tightly in his bedding, seeming very peaceful. Mia nodded and fell to her own dreamless slumber soon enough.

Trin walked away from his concealed place in the shadows and back to his cave, thinking how ironic it was that his past came to haunt him in the form of a girl and how she connected his past to the future for everybody.

Chapter 10: "Lead the Way!"

Trin walked out of the mountain cave as the two young travelers were having breakfast. "Shall we get started then?" he asked them, clapping and rubbing his hands together in anticipation.

Ben scowled, and Mia, who hadn't eaten much that morning, nodded silently. They stood up as Katie poked her head out of Mia's bag. "Who're you?" she asked Trin loudly.

Mildly surprised, Trin's eyebrows went straight up, and he smiled. "My name is Trin. Who might you be, Elf?"

Katie smiled. "Katie, Ben and Mia's friend and the Ice Elf of the Tancredo Maze, not much of a title, I'm afraid." She crawled out and clambered up onto Mia's shoulder. "What are we doing?"

Mia looked at Trin. "We're going to help him get the travelers out of here," she answered.

"Travelers?"

"Yeah, people were on their way somewhere and got stuck here."

"So, how are we going to do this?"

"Magic. Trin's helping us help him." Mia grimly set Katie on Ben's shoulder and stepped forward.

Nodding, Trin pulled her toward a wide open spot by her elbow. "You, with my direction, are going to make a large light beacon. People will be able to see it easily from miles away, and they'll come to investigate." Swallowing nervously, he nodded again, as if reassuring himself. "I thought all night about how we could do this without putting too much strain on your abilities."

Taking a deep breath, Mia allowed herself to be placed carefully on a flat, open piece of ground. Trin stepped back, leaving her alone, standing on a small, completely uncovered spot on the ground. Whispering, Trin told her, "Concentrate on what you want. Nothing else. Imagine wanting it. Grab onto that thread of desire. Make it come closer and closer until you have it inside you, and then let it out."

Mia took a steadying breath and did as he said. *A beacon. A beacon that will bring everyone who sees it closer. That the light is the most important thing right now.* There was a fine fragment of what Mia wanted, drawing slowly and steadily closer in her mind's eye. The closer it came, the more Mia felt it in her soul. There was a part of her that had lain dormant until now, waiting for her to come into her powers for the first time and to acknowledge them. *I'm yours.* Flinging her arms out wide, Mia allowed that feeling to swallow her up and take hold of her.

Ben felt the wind pick up slowly and steadily. Looking around in recognition and worry, he tucked Katie into the hood of his jacket. Backing up against Nomis, Ben kept an eye on Mia and Trin. Trin had a worried expression stamped broadly across his face that was growing more visible by the second, but he didn't move away from Mia. Instead, he motioned Ben forward again.

When Mia flung out her arms, she conjured a wide beam of golden light that shot straight into the air for all to see. She stood before it, her arms falling to her sides and her eyes closing, and she was swaying back and forth, about to fall.

Rushing forward, Ben caught her just before she hit the ground. He would have had a feeling of déjà vu, but Mia's head was rolled back and her eyes were still closed. To the relief of all three, Katie, Ben, and Trin, she was still breathing, even if she was completely unconscious.

Relieved, Ben slumped over, too happy for words that she was all right. Then he looked up, angry, and glared at Trin. "What happened? You said she would be fine!" He shouted.

Trin nodded, taking a deep sigh of relief himself. "She is okay, just sleeping is all. Set her down while we wait. She could use the rest." He began to pace, watching the surrounding mountains for any sign of approaching travelers.

Ben, still glaring, set Mia down and sat beside her. He kept an eye on Trin for a while. When he finally relaxed a little, he shifted Mia's head onto his lap so that she would be more comfortable. Straightening her onyx hair around her face, he smiled to himself. She looked extremely untroubled when she slept.

* * * *

King Dimitri drummed his fingers on the desk. He needed to yell at someone. Knowing the perfect candidate, someone who was afraid of virtually everyone, he roared to the air around him, "Quimble!" He waited impatiently in the short time it took for a trembling, bespectacled man to come through the door. "What took you so long, Quimble?"

"Sorry, Sire," Quimble mumbled semi-apologetically. He bowed humbly before the king, his whole frame wracked in fearful tremors.

"Quimble, go and get me the report from the Captain of the Guard about ... What are you staring at?" he asked angrily. He was unaccustomed to being ignored, but that was exactly what he was receiving from the man that was normally too frightened to do any such thing.

Quimble had straightened and glanced out the transparent ice window, where a golden light caught his eye. He had indeed been staring at it, unknowingly ignoring the king. He felt drawn to it, as if he had to go to it or he was going to miss his last chance at freedom.

Mystified, King Dimitri turned around to see why this frightened little man was not hanging on his every word. A maniacal smile broke onto his face as he realized who must have created it. "Quimble, find out where that light's coming from and have the caster brought straight to the castle."

*   *   *   *

Hundreds of travelers had soon shown up, looking confused and dazed, wondering why they had ended up there, why there was suddenly a light to follow, and who had made it.

Trin stood on a portion of the mountain's base that jutted out like a stage. It became obvious that he was going to speak, and he waited as people nudged those around them, notifying them of the man in worn animal skins. "Travelers, you wish to get out of the mountains, and I, too, wish you free. With some help, I have called you here to show you the way so that you may return to your families and wander through these mountains no more!" He looked from face to face, reading their reactions and trying to anticipate them.

Some of the travelers broke into hushed whispers and loud conversations, all overlapping the others and making no sense. Some didn't believe him, but all were willing to listen. One spoke up, "How could you possibly know the way out? We have been searching for the longest time but haven't found it yet!" He frowned and looked around at other travelers for support. A few nodded at him for encouragement, but others shushed him, not caring about the means of escape.

Nodding his understanding, Trin replied calmly, "But I learned one secret of the mountains long ago. They shift in the dark of night by magic. The first mage of Iceworld fled into the mountains with his family, and to avoid being pursued and brought back to his town and hanged, he enchanted the mountains to move silently and swiftly around any wanderers. The path through them is too long to travel in one day and none have made it through so simply."

The same man protested, "Then how are we to get out? If you can't go across in one day, then there's no chance of us getting out."

"Yes, but we are already more than half way through. It won't take a day to go in any direction." Trin smiled knowingly. "I came to the mountains by choice seventeen years ago and have learned well how to navigate them."

The man nodded. "Fine then, my family and I'll come with you. I don't think it will hurt any..." To that, Trin simply nodded and looked to the others gathered there.

None seemed to have any further questions about following him. Most seemed too weary to care much about it either way.

"Ben, would you take Mia and get on your dragon? She can't stay on very well, so she will need you behind her, holding her in place. Since you, too, are on your way out, I can lead you at the same time." Trin said looking into Ben's face, which was still somewhat suspicious.

"All right," he said as he scooped Mia up into his arms and carried her toward the dragon. Climbing on was barely negotiable, and Ben had to set Mia in front of him, as Trin instructed. He nodded darkly to Trin and called, "Lead the way!"

Trin shook his head solemnly and waved at the group of travelers. He moved forward, and they surged, hesitantly at first, behind him. The mountain man walked confidently around small crevices and past shrubbery that grew weakly between the masses of stone. Many of the travelers exchanged looks at times, but they talked very little.

Nomis took off, and most looked behind them to see what had happened, unused to and perhaps a little frightened of the dragon. Ben looked down at them silently and shifted Mia in her seat. Her head lolled to the side and rested against him, her chin tucked against her shoulder.

Fastening his arms a little more securely around her, Ben laid his cheek gently against her hair. Mia sat motionless in front of him. Her black hair was blown out of her face, and she seemed to look down at the walking travelers below.

Ben smiled very, very lightly. He suddenly heard a small noise from their packs. Quickly looking in, he found Katie where she had relocated while waiting to leave, curled up and laughing. "What's so funny?"

Katie stopped laughing abruptly, forcing her face into a serious mask. "Oh nothing, it's just exactly how I knew it would happen..." she said quickly, subsiding back into laughter.

Ben turned red, but didn't loosen his hold of Mia for fear that she would fall. Suddenly a memory struck him, a memory of a small ice sculpture being suspended in the air as they discussed magic. "Katie, did you know this was going to happen?"

Katie looked back up at him. "Yeah, I did!" She nodded enthusiastically. "I'm half Golen," she stated matter-of-factly.

Ben was sure that his jaw now hung open. "Why didn't you tell us?"

Katie looked confused for a minute. "I thought I already did! Huh, I guess not..." She grinned widely. "Well then, you never asked!"

"Uh, no, I think I would remember that." Ben was only a very little bit annoyed. He didn't mind much. Mia was great, and he had wanted the depiction to be true, even then.

"See! It's not such a bad thing!" Katie pointed out happily. She bounced slightly in the bag.

"Yeah, yeah." Ben shook his head lightly. He could see the amazing progress they were making. There was a strand of light showing through in between the mountains. He pushed on Mia's shoulder, trying to wake her up. She merely shifted and slept on.

Katie frowned at Ben. "Well, don't wake her up, Genius! Let her sleep until we land!" She shook her head exasperatedly. "You don't know much about girls, do you?"

Ben grimaced at being ordered around by a four inch tall elf, but he did as she said. Not long after, they reached the outside of the mountains where they found people spilling forth and smiling and sitting on the ground, happy that they were no longer surrounded by stone. Nomis landed, and Ben pulled Mia off gently.

Setting Mia down, Ben shook her lightly. "Mia, c'mon, we're out. Wake up." Mia's eyes flickered lightly and then clamped themselves tightly shut. "Mia, I know you're awake and can hear me. Get up."

Mia groaned. "You pay too close attention, Ben. Why?" Mia grumbled. She sat up wearily and rubbed her eyes. Stretching, she lifted her arms above her head and leaned backward, yawning as she did. Ben watched her for a moment before replying.

"Because we have to reach the king in order to get you… home, remember?" Ben answered, choking on the mention of sending Mia back. He didn't want to see her go; there were few other people that he enjoyed as much as her, even in the little time they'd spent together.

"Yeah. You know, I'm not sure I want to go home anymore. It wasn't that great really. My dad always in one of his fits, me fighting not to let anyone know about it so he won't be locked up, worrying every day and not knowing whether he'll know me the next minute…" She sighed, looking up at Ben with sad eyes. "But you came all this way. I hate to just turn around and go back at this point. It would have all been for nothing." Shrugging, Mia stood up and walked over to Trin as Katie crawled up to her perch on Mia's shoulder. "So it worked?"

Having trouble imagining her home life, Ben got up and followed her over, feeling slightly dazed. He brought himself back to reality in time to hear Trin answer, "Yes, it did."

"Good, I'm glad I was able to do it. Are you coming

with us to Snowsdale? It's probably been a long time since you've been home."

Shaking his head, Trin's answer was cryptic. "No, I won't come out of the mountains again until the blood Royals sit again on the throne." He paused and then went on. "You have a fine natural talent there, Mia. You are like your mother, so strong-willed and determined. You will be a fine ruler one day." He smiled knowingly and walked briskly back into the mountains.

Mia stared after him a moment before his words sunk in. "You knew my mother? How? Trin! What do you mean?" She yelled after him. Running to the edge of the mountains, she found she could barely see him through a cloud of fog.

Trin merely smiled over his shoulder at her and disappeared almost instantly. Ben shivered. "I'd like to know that, too. I thought you didn't come from Iceworld. How could Trin know your mom?"

Mia sighed and shook her head, confused. "No, I've never been here before in my life, and I don't know how he could possibly know my mother."

"Wow, that was weird," Katie voiced, tilting her head to the side.

Mia and Ben turned toward Nomis, planning to mount and be on their way, but they found him surrounded by people, all wanting to stroke a scale.

Ben looked around and smiled. "Wow, I don't think he's ever gotten so much attention at once. C'mon, we'd better break it up before they spoil him." He continued to grin as he pushed his way through the crowd and got on. Mia followed, and the pair of them were bombarded with questions.

"Where are you going?"
"Are you a sorceress?"

"Did you steal this dragon?"

"How could they steal it, you idiot?"

"Why do you have an Ice Elf on your shoulder?"

"How did you make that light?"

"Magic, how else, Jimmy?"

The two riders answered almost all of the questions, but even Mia didn't understand how she had made the light other than the obvious answer of magic. She sighed exasperatedly and rolled her eyes at Ben. Ben laughed and nodded.

"We're on our way to Snowsdale. If you would move out of the way, we have to get going," he said calmly, yet in a voice loud enough to be heard over the din the large group was making.

The travelers backed a great distance away and waited for the great beast before them to lift off. Nomis reared up and spread his wings, raising a giant "Ahhhhh" from the surrounding audience. Taking off, they heard a cheer below them. Looking over the dragon's side, Mia and Ben saw the people below waving and clapping. Katie, waving back, hung off of Mia's coat.

"Bye! Bye! Bye!" she called to them over and over again. Mia waved happily, and Ben just smiled at both Mia's and Katie's antics. They were being more than comical. It was good that they got to enjoy themselves. He was still a little worried about Mia. Perhaps she shouldn't have done that spell, for she still appeared worn out.

Heading northeast, Ben set his sights for the glimmering city of Snowsdale that was waiting for them. It wouldn't be much longer before their journey across Iceworld would be over.

Chapter 11: Captured

Mia, Ben and Katie sat on Nomis, all buried their own thoughts. Quite a few of these thoughts were about how they were almost to their destination and would have to split up.

Katie wriggled in Mia's hood, unable to get comfortable... *I still don't like tight spaces, but the mountains weren't as bad as the maze. There was more room to move around. Trin was nice, kinda weird, but nice. I hope Ben'll stop to see him again when we head back the other way...*

I wonder what's happening at home. I hope Dad isn't worried about me. Though why should he be? I don't know if he realizes that I'm not some crazed hallucination of Mom. Mia shook her head, blinking back the hot tears that came to her eyes. *I can't wait to see Snowsdale. It's probably so beautiful... I'm sure the King will send me back home; I'll be sad to go and miss Ben and Katie so much...*

Why do I listen to Katie? She's not my boss. She may seem to have it under control, but she's just an elf. I can handle being with Mia. His cheeks flamed and he fought the urge to turn around and look at her. *Mia doesn't really want to go, does she? I wish she didn't have to; I don't want to say good-bye. Good-byes are hard enough without it being to a girl that I...* Ben sighed heavily, not allowing himself to finish the thought. *It doesn't matter anyway. She's just going to go home, and then I'll never see her again.* He looked ahead carefully to see if he could catch any glimpse of Snowsdale, though he couldn't quite see it. *I wonder how long this is going to take. It shouldn't be too much farther.*

They didn't have to wait long. Before five minutes had passed, the city became visible as a shiny spark on the horizon. At first none of them realized what it was, but as they got closer, Mia knew exactly what they were looking at.

"It's Snowsdale! Ben, we made it! We're almost there!" Mia exclaimed quietly to avoid giving Ben hearing damage. She looked on in awe as they drew closer to the sparkling city. Even from this distance, she could tell that it was made of complete ice. The milky whiteness and blue showed how thick the walls were, and she felt a small thrill go up her spine at the thought of entering a large city.

Peering at it, Ben's eye's suddenly widened in surprise. "It is!"

Katie looked up and shrugged, unimpressed. "Looks like another shiny town to me. What's so great about it?"

Ben shook his head in disbelief, frowning at Katie but never taking his eyes off the shimmering sight of the capital as it drew closer and closer. "Katie, it's the capital of Iceworld. What's not so great? I've never been here before and Mia definitely hasn't, so let us enjoy it! We'll be seeing the king before long. Mia won't have long to look."

Katie grumbled, crossing her arms, and tried to situate herself more comfortably. "Fine, but don't expect me to like it." She sat back and closed her eyes. Silently, she saw a small scene play out behind her eyelids. From past experiences, she knew it was a premonition, and she didn't like what she saw. Mia stood in a dark room, isolated and unable to contact anybody.

*   *   *   *

"C'mon, men, the mountains are some distance yet!" the Captain of the Guard himself shouted. He faced forward and marched with a small troop behind him. None of the soldiers liked the stories of the mountains, but they marched wearily on, for they had to follow orders or die trying. "Keep the pace back there! We're on the right track. With any luck," he added darkly to himself, "we won't even have to enter the mountains.

The troop had met a few travelers who said they just escaped the mountains with the help of a black-haired girl, though they hadn't stayed for long enough to find out anything about her.

The captain smiled wearily at the thought. *We'll have our girl yet,* he thought. He felt the mission was an unnecessary waste of time and would be glad when it was done.

The troop marched and marched; soon they saw a huge thing flying towards them. Craning his neck and holding his calloused hand over his eyes to shield them from the light, the captain saw that it was an Ice Dragon. The kind of beast that was supposedly extinct and had no business coming to endanger the city he worked so hard to protect.

Looking a little closer, he saw a sight that made his pulse quicken, and he halted his men. "Men, shoot that beast from the sky!" he ordered. On it sat two people; one of the figures had long black hair and the other with short brown. The pair matched the profiles that we're given to him by the men that paid a visit to the men in Tancredo.

The soldiers obeyed and readied their bows. When the bowstrings were released, the arrows sailed through the air, soaring toward their target. All hit their mark.

Ben was still deep in thought as they drew closer to Snowsdale. He still couldn't imagine the parting or the city itself. He had a painful and awkward image of what he expected, but he avoided thinking about it.

Ben was still in this stupor when Nomis screeched and began to plunge downward. At first, Ben didn't know what was going on, and then he saw the soldiers below.

Growling to himself, Ben shouted back to Mia, "Hang on! We're going to crash!" He grabbed onto one of Nomis's spines and clung there, feeling Mia's arms tighten around him in response to his warning.

Alarmed, Mia shouted back as they fell quickly through the air, "Why?!"

"Because Nomis got shot!"

"Who shot him?" Her voice became a shriek as Nomis lurched and tilted in the air, unable to control his freefall, no matter how he flapped.

"Soldiers!"

Mia looked down just before they crashed into the ground. Soldiers were running toward them. Nomis hit the ground and skid for nearly twenty feet before stopping. Snow was shoved out of his way as he came through it, leaving a large rut of cleared, frozen earth.

Iceworld

Scrambling off the dragon's back, Mia and Ben tried to reassure themselves that their scaly friend was all right. "Is he okay?"Mia asked, gasping for breath.

Ben shook his head frantically, unable to think clearly. "I don't know. He's bad enough. Mia, look out!"

Soldiers rushed in on each side. Two of them grabbed Mia by her shoulders and hauled her roughly to her feet. Screaming, she was dragged away, fighting and kicking as she went.

Ben's eyes grew wide in anger, and he threw himself at the soldiers in an attempt to defend her. "Let her go! We haven't done anything!" He looped his arm around a soldier's throat and tackled him.

For a moment he struggled with the soldier, but was overpowered by the stronger man and hit sharply on the head with the back of the soldier's gauntleted hand. Feeling blood run down the side of his face as he fell to his knees and then to the snow covered ground, Ben knew he was losing consciousness and quickly. The last thing he was aware of was Mia screaming his name as she was dragged away by the soldiers. Then he slid into darkness beside the moaning dragon.

Chapter 12:
The Dungeon

Wizard sighed and leaned back against the wall. There was an echoing of something slapping against the stone-like ice just outside her cell. She could hear someone coming down the stairs. *Maybe King Dimitri is ready to let me out already. That will be the shortest time that he's stayed mad at me.* She stood up, brushed some of the dust off her robe and moved closer to the cell door. Listening more closely, she realized that there was more noise than there should be if they really were releasing her.

Backing away from the door, Wizard counted down on her fingers. *Three, two, one.* Right on cue, the door swung open and bashed against the wall behind it, only proving the soldiers' own predictability. The guards threw in a slim-figured girl who got up and rushed at the door, trying to escape before they closed it. She failed; the pack that they hadn't taken from her lay on the ground behind her as she pounded hopelessly on the door.

"You know, that won't help," Wizard told her as the girl banged her fist against the door, sliding back into a sitting position. "The only ones who can hear you are the guards."

The girl spun around, startled. "Who are you?" Her expression was weary and a large bruise had started forming on the side of her face. No doubt she had tried to fight the guards on the way into the castle. The gruff men were known for little patience and short tempers.

"My name is Wizard Wiesemann. What about you?"

"Mia Snow," she answered distractedly. "What is this place?"

Wizard shrugged. "It's the dungeon, what else? It's dark, cold, hard, and isolated. What are you in for?" A small smile tugged at her lips; she'd never had anyone to talk with in the dungeon before.

"I don't know!" Mia started storming around the dungeon, waving her hands through the cool air. "They shot at us and then dragged me in here!" She kicked the wall in frustration, a growl reverberating from her throat.

"The walls are magically enforced. Technically, all of them are, but especially the dungeon's walls." Wizard frowned, unhappy that her company was in no mood to talk. "I was thrown in here for angering the king, again. It's not like I try to make him angry, but he's got a horrible temper and is much too easy to upset!"

Mia nodded. "I would guess so. I don't even know him, and I was thrown into the dungeon!" She slumped to the floor in defeat and sat there with her eyes closed, taking deep breaths. As if to calm herself down, she asked, "Why is King Dimitri so irritable?"

Wizard scooted along the wall to sit beside her. "Well, he's nervous." She placed her hands on her knees and glanced at the cell door to make sure the guards couldn't hear her.

"About what?" Mia opened her eyes and stared ahead, trying to listen to the story.

"He's nervous that he doesn't know what he needs to know. He doesn't know if the Ice Princess is coming home to take her rightful place as the heir to the throne or not."

Mia turned her head to really look at her cellmate, eyes wide, and thoroughly interested. "His daughter?"

Wizard shook her head slowly, her white-blond hair swaying by her ears. "No, his enemy's daughter. She's the sole heir to the throne, and if she returns, she would be extremely powerful and able to rightfully dethrone him." Brow furrowed, she continued in a more pensive voice. "It's been almost eighteen years since she was even thought of..."

"What do you mean?" Mia pressed anxious. She couldn't explain why she was suddenly so caught up in this. Maybe it was because a small part of her wondered that if she understood the king, she'd be able to convince him she meant no harm and that she just wanted to go home.

"Well... she wasn't born yet when her mother and father disappeared." With a glance at Mia's shocked expression, she frowned. "I suppose I had better begin the story at the beginning." Wizard took a deep breath and launched into Iceworld's history.

"I had only been working here a few years when this story starts. Nineteen years ago, the queen-to-be, the 'current' princess's mother, was very stubborn. Her parents were setting up an arranged marriage for her, and that was something that she definitely didn't want.

"The princess was in love with a charming young man from the city. He came to visit whenever he could; though, there was a law that stated very clearly that the princess's suitor must be of noble blood and the marriage was to be arranged by the ruling monarchs. One day, when she couldn't bear the thought of being separated from him anymore, she informed her mother and father that she refused to marry anyone but him. They refused for the longest time before finally giving into their daughter's request.

"At the time, there was only one suitor, and he was a jealous man. He was furious when the king and queen relented and changed the law so that a princess must marry the man her parents chose unless she loves someone else already.

"The suitor learned that he had lost the favor of the royal family and was no longer a candidate for the next king and went absolutely star-craving mad. He disappeared for nearly a year in which nobody could remember hearing from or seeing him. When he came back, the princess's parents had died, and she and her consort were to be crowned the next rulers of Iceworld, but there was no time for a coronation. The rejected suitor drove the couple out once he got news that they were having a daughter. They were forced to flee, not wanting to endanger their unborn daughter. The princess enlisted the help of her brother who helped them escape, but he stayed behind, hiding from civilization until the rightful ruler sits on the throne again.

"The suitor took over, crowning himself the new king, and vowed that he would get the family back if it was the last thing he ever did in his life. As far as I know, they haven't shown their faces around here again. For good reason, I suppose," Wizard sighed. "I wish they would come back. That baby girl is probably all grown up, and she's bound to look just as beautiful and regal as her mother."

Confused, Mia started to ask a question and then held back.

"What is it?" Wizard asked, remembering that she had an audience.

"It's just, how did you know it was a baby girl if she hadn't been born yet?"

"The Royal physicians usually have someone among them who knows magic, or they have one of the Counsel of Magic help out. There's really a simple process to find that sort of information out."

Mia nodded. "How will you know the Princess if she does come back?" she asked, interested.

Wizard gave her a small, knowing smile. "The Princess wears a special necklace in the shape of a snowflake. It was handed down from generation to generation to the first born princess in the family.

"The necklace itself is special. It never tarnishes, so it will always stay bright silver. When it was created, it was thought that the snowflake would embody the image of Iceworld."

Mia's eyes grew wider in the gloom, seeming to shine white. "A- a snowflake?" Her hand flew to her own neck where her mother's necklace hung.

"Yes, that's just what I said. It was fitting for the female ruler of Iceworld has something significant to show who she is. Though, no one really knows if it's been passed down now."

Mia fell silent. Thinking rapidly, there seemed to be no other solution. No one in her hometown remembered her parents before they had her, only that they had moved to town with a small daughter and wouldn't tell anyone from where. Her mother and father had truly relished summer and were indifferent to winter. Then there was the necklace; that alone would offer some sort of proof. "Couldn't someone else wear a snowflake necklace?" she asked anxiously, looking for anything to shatter the train of thought that was wiggling its way into her mind.

Wizard shook her head, her face wrinkled in doubt. "No, there is only one necklace like hers in existence, and it was made by the most talented sorcerer. Taking a snowflake and freezing it in place quickly is such a delicate process that no other magician has managed it. It was only done by bonding the essence of Iceworld and the first princess's innocence."

Swallowing harshly, Mia nodded sat with her knees curled up to her chest, on the dungeon floor without saying a thing. She seemed to have retreated inside her own mind, and Wizard left her alone for a while.

Some hours later dinner came, and the two cellmates ate silently. Wizard, growing bored and impatient, decided to get rid of some of her questions about this mysterious girl. "Where do you come from?"

Mia shifted uncomfortably. "Not from Iceworld, at least, I didn't think I was."

"You're not sure?" She joked half-heartedly before realizing from Mia's closed off expression that she didn't want to expound on that subject any further. "You said that you were traveling with someone?"

"Yes. He's a friend of mine, Ben," Mia answered. What could it hurt to tell her that? It wasn't like she was able to go track him down anyway.

"Where did you start your journey?"

"Um, we started at the southern edge of Iceworld. I think he said it was close to Mabec.

"Where were you headed?"

"We were on our way to speak with the king."

Startled, Wizard's eyes widened as she asked in a hushed whisper, "Why?"

"Because I wanted to go home," Mia said a little agitated. "Is that so hard to understand? It doesn't seem like much of an option anymore, though." She shook her head and put the remainder of her food back and the metal tray that it had been brought to them on.

"Why not?" Wizard asked cautiously, knowing she was starting to get on the girl's delicate nerves.

"Because I'm locked up in a dungeon, with no way out, and the king doesn't seem to like me very well!" Mia half yelled, frustrated.

A guard poked his head through the door, peering at them in the dim light. They hushed, afraid they were about to be reprimanded for yelling, but he continued into the room and stood threateningly over Mia. "King Dimitri has ordered to see the Ice Princess," he informed them rigidly...

Mia got to her feet and followed the soldier to the door. She glanced apologetically back at Wizard, who seemed too dumbfounded for words, before stepping out the door after the guard.

There were two burly, uniformed men waiting for her just outside the door. She was grabbed roughly by the arms and half marched, half dragged up the stairs that she had been shoved down in what seemed like such a long time ago.

It appeared as if the guards weren't happy about pointlessly dragging some teenager up and down the stairs either. They never said a word to indicate such a thing, but the stiff and bored way they were walking suggested that they wanted something better to do.

Iceworld

They walked for a long time, up and up, around and around, until they finally came upon a large door engraved all sorts of pictures, but it wasn't the markings on the door that drew Mia's attention. The guard standing outside was green, his hands webbed, resembling, more than anything, a frog.

Barely able to restrain a smile, Mia waited anxiously for whatever was going to happen to begin. The guards nodded to their frog-like comrade before opening the door for Mia, pushing her inside. Walking in, she found thousands of shelves lined with books, long tables set next to high windows for the light, and in one of the cushy chairs that surrounded each table, at the closest table sat a tall man, scrutinizing her with his fingertips touching each other as he held them up to his lips.

Chapter 13: The King

The man in the chair smiled at her in an obvious attempt to be warm. "Welcome to my study, Princess." He stood and came closer to her, his pale blond hair shining white in the soft light.

Standing absolutely still, Mia watched this man nervously, scared about what he wanted with her. If she was the Ice Princess, he had sworn to 'get' her family back, but just how far was he willing to go? Would he try and kill her here? Now?

King Dimitri stopped directly in front of her and examined her for a moment. He contemplated everything about her, her black hair, blue eyes, snowflake necklace, and finally the bruise that covered almost half of her face. Taking her chin in his hand, he turned her head to look at this feature more carefully, as if trying to tell what she would look like beneath the bruise.

Mia cleared her throat loudly, shifting uneasily from one foot to the other. She pulled away from this unsettling man enough for his hand to drop to his side.

The king shook his head and returned to his senses. "I apologize. I shouldn't keep my guests waiting so long. Please, sit." Saying each word deliberately, he gallantly pulled out a chair for her. The slippery smoothness of his voice reminded Mia greatly of oil, slow, thick, oozing, and dangerous.

Sitting in the chair cautiously, Mia frowned, making her bruise ache. "I wasn't aware that you threw guests into the dungeon so roughly," she retorted, trying to seem confident and cynical. "Where I come from, they're welcomed with open arms and shown every luxury that can be afforded."

For a moment, his mask of a warm, comforting host slipped. Reasserting himself, King Dimitri shook his head, his jovial smile back in place. "Of course not. I apologize deeply for that. I wasn't aware that it was you I sent down there. If I had been informed that one so highly respected as you was coming to see me, I would have opened my doors and welcomed you immediately. Although, you have to forgive my soldiers, they thought you might be part of a rebellion. One can never be too careful." He smiled soothingly at her. "I hear you were seen riding toward the city on a dragon. Imagine how alarmed they must have been."

Mia nodded stiffly. "I suppose." She watched as the king sat back down in his seat. His movements were fluid and confident with a practiced air.

"I know that, as Princess, you're very powerful. If you had wanted to, I would imagine that you probably could have left the dungeon without any need to send the guards to release you," he continued smoothly. "Magic is a very handy thing in that it can't be contained, just controlled."

In this, Mia knew there was dishonesty hidden in his slippery voice. "You know," she began in a soft voice, "I met a woman named Wizard Wiesemann in the dungeon. She told me that no one could get out of the dungeon from the inside."

King Dimitri expression became blank momentarily as he contemplated this piece of information. Finally, he smiled again and nodded deeply. "Well, that's Wiesemann for you. She is quite incompetent. Did you notice the guard outside the door? Yes, I suppose you did. That's Wiesemann's work. She never finished the frog spell and ended up with some cross-mixed, mutated guard. Only the crowned rulers and royal family have such power as we do, Mia. She probably only knows that people with normal powers have no chance of escaping."

Mia didn't respond. Instead, she simply looked around at the innumerable books that surrounded them and avoided looking at the king. She no longer knew whether he was lying or not.

She could feel his eyes roaming over her face before King Dimitri opened his mouth to speak. "Other than the bruise, you look so like your mother. Pity she couldn't be here, too. But you're here with me now, aren't you? Would you honor me with your name?" he asked innocently.

Mia shook her head. "I would; it's Mia," she told him shortly. His comment on her mother made Mia's stomach flip. "How do you know I'm who you think I am?"

The king nodded. "Mia, I could sense the power coming from you, and the necklace is unmistakable. Its painted likeness hangs on a wall of this very room."

He paused, eyeing the mark of power that hung on such a delicate silver chain, before continuing along a different line. "I have to admit that I didn't call you here just to reminisce about your family. I brought you here because I would like to speak to you about your future here at the palace."

"I wasn't aware that I had a future here," Mia interrupted callously. She sat back against her chair and glared at the king with a carefully guarded expression, arms crossed against her chest.

"It's very possible," King Dimitri told her, returning her gaze firmly. Some hidden emotion was concealed behind his eyes. There was something he wanted from this young girl, and he wasn't going to be very happy if he didn't get it. "Well, you see, I won't be around forever. As of yet, I have no heir. I need someone who will take over easily when I die, someone with magic coursing through his or her veins—"

"Someone like me," Mia finished, surprised. She hadn't been expecting an offer like this. Her thoughts returned to the honest, frank conversation she'd had with Wizard and frowned. "Well, I've heard the story about how you took power. Why would someone want to make their enemy's daughter his sole heir?" she questioned him experimentally, gauging his reaction.

The king's eyebrows shot up in surprise, and his expression darkened almost imperceptibly. In response to this, Mia smiled and suddenly knew that she had the upper-hand, "I find it odd that you would want such a thing. If you swore to get retribution against my mother and father for cheating you out of the crown, you wouldn't want to put me in power. It'd be like giving the crown back to them after all this time, giving it back to the rightful King and Queen of Iceworld!" Her words came sharp and fast. She suddenly realized that the King was scowling at her but said nothing.

"Then, you will respect my decision to decline your offer. For some reason, I think you had something to do with the way I was raised. For instance, the reason I didn't grow up in Iceworld or how my life has been all but happy for the last ten years."

The king's face had grown darker, his eyes becoming narrower and narrower with every second that passed. "But haven't you wondered why your mother died so suddenly or why your father is certifiably insane? Why you've had to hide from him in fear of what he may do to you?" he snarled, his voice shaking with anger.

Mia grew pale. "How did you kn---" Something clicked and she found herself staring at her mother's murderer with an expression of pure horror. "It was you, wasn't it? You killed her? You did that to them?!" she asked, her voice rising in hysteria.

Cold laughter filled the room. The king stood and placed his palms on the table, leaning toward her threateningly. "Oh, very perceptive. Yes, it was me. I sent a curse after the wretched couple. They deserved what they got...

"It wasn't easy, of course not, but necessary. I couldn't have them coming back to reclaim the throne. Something of theirs was needed for the full effect of the spell. I had a whole castle full of things of your mother's. Your father was more difficult; he never brought much to the castle and took most of his belongings with him when they left. I did manage to track down a small item in his room, however." The king's grin was bloodthirsty and menacing. Mia found herself leaning as far away from him as her seat would allow.

"The biggest problem, however, was you. You hadn't been born yet when they left, so there was nothing that belonged to you, nothing that could have been used to send the curse after you; therefore, you remained untouched by it."

He laughed his spine-chilling cackle again. "Diane, your mother," he spat out the words as if they would contaminate the air, "couldn't possibly take all of her things with her. It was really too easy to find a thing that had enough of her to take her life. Simon wasn't as greatly affected, but it was strong enough that he could never return."

Shaking with untempered rage, Mia knocked her chair over with a muffled crash as she stood up. She seemed to radiate the heat of her hatred. She desperately didn't want him to know that he had gotten to her, so she stayed silent.

Despite her efforts, King Dimitri knew from the way she was clenching her jaw and fists that he had struck a nerve. Coolly, looking at his nails disinterestedly, he drawled, "So, how did you like growing up in the arms of a lunatic?"

The last sane, sensible part of her snapped. Screaming at him, she picked up her chair and hurled at him.

The king lazily raised a hand and, with the force of his magic, managed to deflect it before it reached him. Glowering at him, with tears streaming down her face, Mia started shouting all the unsavory things that came to mind.

Gazing at Mia disdainfully, King Dimitri raised an eyebrow at her. "You should really watch your language girl. I think a few days back in the dungeon will help that foul mouth you have there." Mia's vision started going fuzzy and she blinked several times to no avail. "Do say hello to

Wiesemann for me, won't you?"

Mia blinked again but, instead of the Royal Study, found herself in the dark, unlit dungeon again. Shocked, she looked around to a mildly surprised Wizard, who was staring at her from her seat against the wall, knees tucked to her chest.

"So," Wizard said, seeming perfectly at ease, "How'd it go?"

Chapter 14: Plans

"I'm not sure what he was doing, telling you that," Wizard repeated. "He knows very well that this cell was designed for magic users, specifically strong ones. Not even all of the mages in Iceworld together could have broken out of here using magic." She paused, huffing in indignation. "Incompetent, humph, I'll show him incompetent," she grumbled. Sighing, she shook her head and looked at Mia, ready to explain. "Anyone who tries to use magic from the inside of this particular cell will be drained physically and mentally. If they keep trying to break out, the strength of the magic that laces the walls in here will eventually kill them."

Mia kicked the wall in frustration with left-over rage from her encounter with the king, making her toe throb. "So, everything he said was a lie?" she asked angrily, not looking at Wizard, wanting the effect on her father to be reversible.

Wizard shrugged noncommittally. "Oh, I wouldn't put it past him to actually send a curse after your parents. I guess the only upside of all this is that you know who you're parents were and where you're from," she pointed out optimistically.

Seeing Mia's less than enthusiastic expression, she added, "The only advice I can really give you is don't give into him and don't keep pushing him over the edge like that. I don't know what he's planning, but it can't be good, especially when you consider who we're dealing with. Making him angrier won't help your situation."

Nodding reluctantly, Mia sat down. "So, now what?"

There was no response, as if Wizard hadn't heard her. "Wizard?" She turned to see what was wrong with her cellmate and found that she was sitting stock-still, staring over Mia's shoulder at something. "What's in your bag?" she asked carefully.

Mia looked over at her pack that had been carelessly thrown into the cell and left where it had fallen. It was shifting slightly. Wizard was apparently afraid, perhaps, that it might be a rat or some other unpleasant, small animal.

Crawling over to the pack, Mia undid the flap and opened it up. A very small figure came rolling out of the opening. "Katie?"

The Ice Elf looked up, eyes wide and surprised. "Yeah," looking around and taking in the very little detail there was, added, "Where are we?"

Mia picked the elf up and sat so that her back was against the wall, setting Katie on her knee so that they could talk easier. "We got thrown into the king's dungeon.

Were you in my pack the entire time? You've been awfully quiet. We never heard a thing."

Katie glared up at her. "No, I came in through the door. They were really nice." Scowling, she settled down on Mia's knee. Did we really get 'thrown' in here? 'Cause my head hurts. I mighta hit my head on the floor when the bag landed," she replied, rubbing her head for effect.

"Sounds like it hurt, but there wasn't anything I could do. If I had known you were in there, I would have made more of an effort to help, though." She gave the elf a reproachful look before waving a casual hand in Wizard's direction. "This is Wizard Wiesemann, by the way," she introduced them, spotting the baffled look on Wizard's face. "Wizard, this is Katie. She's an Ice Elf that I've been traveling with."

Wizard inclined her head. "Good to meet you, Katie. Maybe you could help us think of a way out of here. So far we've had no luck."

Katie nodded sharply and quickly, so much so that it looked like it must have hurt. "Sure, but we might want to get a hold of Ben. He's still out there and probably worried. He might even be able to help!" She raised her hands as she had when conjuring the ice sculpture back when Mia had used magic to find her mother's necklace, and a shimmering illusion soon hovered in front of their faces.

Wizard started violently, crawling closer to them to get a better look at what Katie was doing. "You can do magic in here?" she asked, shocked.

Katie, not gathering the meaning of her question, was very confused and nodded slowly. "Yeah, I can do magic just about anywhere," she responded.

Mia chuckled. "This dungeon is impervious to magic. It supposedly kills any magic user trying to escape." Turning to Wizard, she grinned widely. "Katie, If you can do magic in here, we might have a chance to escape!" she told her quietly but excitedly, not wanting to alert the guards to any of their plotting.

Katie nodded, understanding. "Sounds good, but we still need to contact Ben." A dark figure started to form and became clearer within the icy haze.

"Of course," Mia said, nodding. She looked at the figure, with Wizard crowding in beside her, and found Ben's form coming into sharp relief.

* * * *

Ben was poking at a fire with some of the wood that he'd managed to find. Nomis groaned behind him, shifting to get in a less painful position. Turning to check on him, Ben shook his head sadly, wondering what he'd do with the injured dragon. He'd barely managed to calm Nomis down enough to jerk the arrows out without being knocked twenty feet back. Half of the arrows had come with sickening squelches or tearing sounds from the skin in between the scales that were fighting to heal over nasty gashes.

Nomis was lying where he'd landed, gently licking the injured flesh. Avoiding the gruesome sight, Ben faced his fire once more, his face tight. Looking up, he fell backward into the snow with a yelp of surprise. A shimmering haze hovered in front of him, and in it were Mia, Katie and a woman that he'd never seen before.

Standing back up, Ben smeared some of the snow in his face. *I must be dreaming. Mia was captured by the guard. There's no way I'm seeing her right now. I don't even know what happened to Katie*, he added in his thoughts. *They're just part of my imagination. I've just been hiding out with only a dragon for company for way too long now.*

"Ben, can you hear us?" Mia's voice asked gently, gauging the connection. He was convinced that he wouldn't be able to come up with the sound of her musical, lilting voice saying those words. So, looking up, Ben was relieved to see that the trio was still there, hovering before him and watching him anxiously. "Ben?"

Shaking himself, Ben realized that she was waiting for him to say something and steeled himself to answer. "I'm here, and I can hear you just fine. So, I'm definitely *not* dreaming?" he asked, just to be sure.

Mia's face twisted slightly in confusion. "No, of course not. What made you think that?" Waving a hand in dismissal, she turned to the most pressing matter at hand. "Never mind, Katie's here and is keeping the connection going for as long as we need. This is Wizard Wiesemann, King Dimitri's Head Magician. We're in the dungeon."

Nodding, Ben chuckled grimly. "Yeah, I kinda guessed that, since the guards literally hauled you away. Are you all right? I heard you yell my name before I blacked out," he explained gingerly, wanting more than anything for her to be okay. He could already see a huge bruise on her face.

Mia smiled softly. "Yes, I'm fine. I was worried for you; you looked so hurt, but there wasn't a lot I could do to help you." She paused. "Look, Ben, I need to condense this for you, but please don't ask any questions; we'll have time for them later if this works. I'm the long lost Ice Princess. The king drove my parents from Iceworld before I was born and sent a curse after them, killing my mom and driving my father insane. Now he's after me. We have to get out of here, and we need your help to do it."

Ben's jaw dropped open, and, though Mia had asked him not to, he couldn't resist asking a question or two. He held up his hand to stop her. "You're a princess? Our princess? Whoa... Wait, you said that king's magician is right there with you? Why can't you just have her persuade him to let you go?" he asked, trying to find a simple way to help.

"Because, I'm in the dungeon too, for a reason or two: he's not happy with me and I'm not his favorite advisor anyway," Wizard pitched in, her feelings on the matter still a little heated. "You weren't supposed to ask questions," she added snappishly.

"Oh, right, sorry," Ben apologized.

"Ben, we can get out of here with Katie's help, but we need a quick and easy get-away," Mia stated as if she planned for breaking out of prison everyday of her life.

Ben nodded. "I understand, but Nomis is really badly hurt. He barely managed to stay calm long enough for me to get the arrows out of him, and he can't move, let alone fly, without hurting himself. There's just no way."

Wizard's eyebrows shot up, and her disapproval and horror showed clearly on her face. "King Dimitri was willing to take this farther than I thought. Who's Nomis?"

"Our dragon," Mia answered briefly before turning back to Ben. "Is he going to be all right?"

"Well, he's alive," Ben said, shrugging. "He'll get better eventually. So, how are you guys planning on getting out of there?"

Chapter 15: Escape

King Dimitri shuffled through his papers impatiently. He was preparing his own plans for his prisoners in cell one. "Quimble!"

The quivering man stumbled to the king's side, fearful as ever. "Y-- Yes, Sire?" He trembled at the sound of King Dimitri's impatient voice. Since the king had met with the young woman he held as prisoner, he'd been even colder and more venomous than before, though no one knew it was possible.

"Stop your shaking and go fetch any magic books that mention draining humans," King Dimitri answered coldly without looking up, irritation edging his voice to a sharp point.

All color drained from Quimble's face. "B- But, Sire, those spells could kill someone! W-- Why do you want *them?"*

The king's anger burst. "Who cares *why*, Quimble? Just do it or you'll be spending a lot of time together with Wiesemann in the dungeon!" he bellowed at the man who was backing quickly out of the room.

Quimble soon returned with an armful of books. They were all bound in black leather and possessed silver enamel on the spines. "Here, S--Sire," he said, placing them on the table, a few landing on the floor with a heavy *THUD*. Picking up the few that he had dropped, Quimble bowed low and left the room before the king could order him about anymore.

Outside in the corridor, Quimble relaxed slightly and took a deep breath to calm his agitated nerves. He felt a twinge of sympathy for the Ice Princess. Wizard had once explained to him that when a sorcerer drained someone of his or her magical ability, it was worse than killing the poor person. A soul would be left, barely hanging onto the body, drained of more than half of itself. The victim would die shortly afterward, unable to maintain life for more than an hour in his or her empty shell of a body. It seemed a very dark thing indeed to do to him, and he made a mental note not to be around when it happened.

Deciding to find out what had become of Wizard in the dungeon, Quimble drifted down toward the many flights of steps, avoiding the gaze of everyone he passed. Sometime later, he pushed open the door to the dungeon. "Wizard?" he called softly into the gloom.

"Quimble?" came the shocked reply in the familiar voice, "What are you doing down here?" Wizard asked, standing up so that he could see her better as his eyes adjusted slowly to the dim lighting. "Don't tell me the king chucked you in here as well."

Iceworld

"I-- I came down to see how you were. The king said you were in the dungeon, so..." his voice trailed off as a movement to his right caught his attention. A young woman stepped forward, examining him carefully. A large bruise covered half of her face, and he knew exactly who it was.

Wizard followed his gaze. "Oh, I'm sorry. This is Mia, the Ice Princess. Mia, this is Quimble, another one of the other servants the king rules by fear," she said, introducing them.

Mia shared a small smile with him. "Nice to meet you, Quimble, though we *are* in the middle of some unfortunate circumstances." She shot an anxious look at Wizard, who nodded reluctantly.

Quimble, growing uneasy from the women's exchange, took a step back. "Yes, indeed. Unfortunate they are," he squeaked. They were now looking at him apologetically and walking slowly and deliberately toward him.

In a moment, Wizard and Mia had grabbed him, and Katie, unnoticed from Mia's shoulder, froze Quimble's jaw so that he couldn't yell for help to the guards who remained just outside the door.

"Please forgive us," Wizard whispered to him before pushing him farther into the cell and swinging the door wide.

Wizard jumped into the hall and petrified the guards; they wouldn't know that the trio escaped until Quimble's jaw thawed out and they had safely gotten away, hopefully. "C'mon," she whispered to Mia, running up the stairs.

Mia followed after her, with her bag slung over one shoulder and Katie on the other. With Wizard leading the way, they crept through several corridors until they finally had a chance to contact Ben again without getting caught.

"Ben, we're out of the dungeon," Mia told him

solemnly.

Ben's eyebrow's shot up in mild surprise. "Well, that was fast. I thought you were going to wait for someone to bring in the food tray."

Mia shrugged. "Well, turns out that we didn't have to wait that long for a different opportunity. We had a visitor; he's locked in the dungeon now."

"The king?" Ben asked in a shocked voice, thinking that sounded like the answer to their problems.

"*No*! Do you really think we'd be able to lock up King Dimitri? We'll probably be out of the palace and the city in about a half an hour," Mia informed him.

"All right, I'll be waiting here, as if I have anything better to do," he added, rolling his eyes.

Mia laughed, waved good-bye, and let Katie end the connection. She watched as Wizard peered cautiously around the corner. "Is the coast clear?"

Wizard made a face, deciding. "Well, there's a guard standing directly in front of the door that we need to go through. From there, we'll be able to go straight to the main entrance. It's a short cut of some sort," Wizard replied in a hushed tone.

"So, what should we do?" Mia asked.

Wizard turned and looked straight at Katie, and her thoughts were obvious. "Well…"

Katie's shoulders slumped. "What do you want me to do?" she asked, her voice resigned.

*   *   *   *

Several minutes later, Katie was running through the hall. Heading straight for the dumbfounded guard, who was staring at her as if he just couldn't believe his eyes, she quickly created a chunk of ice in her hand. Aiming carefully, she threw it, hitting the guard squarely on the nose, and sped down the hall and out of sight around a corner. Shaking his head and swiping at his nose, he yelled and ran after her. He dashed around the corner, hot on the elf's heels. Before long, Katie had eluded him and hurried back to the door with Wizard and Mia.

Before slipping quietly through the door, Mia scooped up the little elf and placed her back on her usual perch on the girl's shoulder.

"Thanks, Katie," she whispered. Wizard continued to lead them through the winding corridors, and Mia started to wonder how long it would have taken them to escape without the "shortcut." It occurred to her at some point that she should be suspicious of Wizard. She was the king's magician after all. She could have been planted in the dungeon to gain her confidence and find something out that they could use against her. She brushed the thought off, however. If Wizard was really working for the king, why would the king have arranged for her to help her "escape"?

At last, they reached the final door, Wizard stopped them. "There's a huge training ground on the other side of this door. On the far side, there's a gate that leads out of the palace walls and into the city. If we can make it that far, we should be able to make it out of here with no other problems. I'm going to set an enchantment that will help us slip right past them. No one will be able to see us, but remember that just because they can't see us, doesn't mean they can't feel or hear us," she warned. Wizard closed her eyes and concentrated. Mia could feel the magic rolling over her and suddenly the magician's outline became fuzzier and blurred in her vision and then disappeared altogether. Looking down, she realized that the same thing had happened to her and Katie. The door creaked open just a little bit, and she heard Wizard's disembodied voice whisper, "Let's get going."

Slipping through the door, Mia saw rows upon rows of perhaps a few hundred soldiers, all learning different skills. Mia, unable to see Wizard, was forced to weave her own way in between the disciplined soldiers. On the far side of the enormous courtyard was a large gate. The two doors stood tall and loomed over everyone inside and out.

They were almost to the other side of the courtyard when they found a battalion of young men, learning the basics of marching. They followed their commands to a T, turning on their heels and facing all sorts of directions.

Mia, misjudging the focus of one particular guard, walked forward and stumbled into him when he failed to stop and turn with such precision. Tumbling to the ground, she shrieked, remembering too late that she could still be heard.

The guard had been day-dreaming of the days before he'd been torn away from his happy life at home to serve in the army when something crashed into him with a scream. Wildly, he looked around in shock, trying to see what it was that had careened into him with such force. Seeing nothing in the dimming daylight of the evening, he cautiously felt around on the ground with his foot.

Mia felt his foot travel around her arm and head; it was enough that he realized that he could feel a person. He ran from the spot, sounding the alert to the other guards. Getting up, Mia practically flew towards the gates. She could still feel Katie on her shoulder, so she didn't pause to find the elf.

The gate was open when she finally managed to reach it. Wizard's spell was definitely wearing off, and Mia could see the hazy figure of the woman helping her escape. She was sure the same was happening to her and Katie, but she didn't take the time to check.

"We need to leave! They know we've escaped!" She shouted to Wizard on her way past. Dashing through the gate, Mia tried to remember where Ben said Nomis had crashed. The information presented itself at the front of her mind, and she ran in the direction, waving for Wizard to follow.

Picking up her pace, Mia kept going, desperate to get away from the walls of the city. As she sprinted by, she noticed a poster materializing. Pausing and out of breath, Mia stopped in front of it and her eyes widened as she read it. Groaning, she watched as Wizard drew even with her, and she took off again, leading the way to where she could vaguely remember the dragon and her friend being. Behind her, she could hear a great, tolling bell ring in the castle, warning the city and the guards in it to beware of the fugitives.

"It seems-- as if-- we don't have-- as much time-- as we-- hoped," Wizard panted beside her.

Mia nodded and kept running. Soon they were at the outskirts of the city, and Mia could clearly see Ben standing by Nomis, waving at them to hurry. When they came close enough, they slowed down and walked the short distance left. Wizard went straight to Nomis to immediately heal his wounds, as they had planned. With any luck, he would be able to fly again in a few short minutes.

Mia ignored everything and threw her arms around Ben's neck and hugged him tightly. Ben turned red but hugged her back, squeezing her as if afraid to let go.

"I worried that I wouldn't ever see you again or that I'd have to go in there and break you out myself," he told her, joking half-heartedly. He ignored Katie who was laughing silently in Mia's hood, where she'd fallen during the sprint.

"I didn't have much hope either. We couldn't have gotten out without Katie's help, or Wizard's," Mia replied, pulling away.

Releasing her, Ben stepped back to the remains of his fire. He kicked snow over them and grabbed his pack and Mia's off her shoulder and proceeded to tie them to Nomis's back, being careful not to disturb Wizard. The king's magician was kneeling at the dragon's side with her eyes squeezed shut in concentration. If she was doing something, Ben couldn't tell, but he didn't want to accidentally interrupt her.

"I don't know if Nomis can hold three," he said shortly. "He shouldn't have any problem, but there's no telling how long he can fly. He's never *had* to carry three before."

"Well, he's going to have to now," Mia retorted shortly. "Both Wizard and I are fugitives from the king. I saw a 'Wanted' poster in the city," she added. "We both fall under the headline: 'Wanted for Treason.'"

Wizard turned, bristling. "What? That's horrible! I served the royal family, the king, and everyone in the palace for twenty years and this is how they react when I get out of prison? And I've done nothing treasonous!" she declared, outraged.

Mia shrugged. "They don't seem to care at this point, and there's no going back to correct them. We have to get out of here!" she reinforced, glancing at Nomis, who was completely healthy again and was stretching his wings and standing on his feet again.

Wizard nodded, deflating slightly. "Right, of course. Let's go."

Ben climbed onto Nomis, Mia following him with a nervous Wizard just behind her. Nomis flapped his wings with renewed vigor. His take off was shaky, but they remained firmly in the air. The fugitives saw soldiers streaming out of the palace gates, pointing and shouting in their direction. Ben quickly directed Nomis back toward the looming mountains.

"Hopefully Trin will let us back in. The mountains will slow down the soldiers," he called back over the wind as Katie started the icy haze that allowed them to communicate with the mountaineer.

Mia nodded. "I hope so, too." When Trin appeared in the haze, he seemed a little puzzled as he stared back out at them. "Trin?"

Answering back with very little shock in his voice, Trin smiled. "Yes, Mia?"

"We are on the run from the king's soldiers. Would you be willing to come back to the edge of the mountains and lead us in to hide from them, please?" Mia asked, straining to be heard over the rush of wings.

"Of course; you can stay here with me; I'll be there when you arrive," he said with a note of finality. Katie let his image and the haze disappear.

The group flew safely to the mountains, met Trin and went to his cave. Trin showed them into the tunnels, taking them to a type of side chamber, and told them that in the morning, when they woke up, they needed to go to the central chamber. He gave them directions and told them that for that night, they would all sleep right there.

Chapter 16: Explanations

Mia shifted to get more comfortable, the arm around her shoulders moving with her. Groggily, she realized that she was leaning on someone's shoulder and felt an arm around her. Her eyes popped open and sat up abruptly. Looking beside her, she saw Ben reclined against the wall, sound asleep. Last night she'd been sitting beside him, repeating Wizard's story about her parents and the king, and she must have dozed off, leaning against him in her sleep.

The chamber was empty apart for the two of them. Since it seemed like the adults had left them to sleep, Mia shook Ben to wake him up. "Ben, c'mon. Get up, sleepyhead," she called to him. When he failed to get up, she pushed him over and watched as he started to stir on the cold, rocky ground.

Ben's eyelids flickered open. Rubbing the warm spot on his shoulder where Mia's head had recently been lying, he sat up and peered at her through bleary eyes. "What's up?"

"We have to find the main cave. Wizard and Trin are already gone," she replied distantly.

As Ben woke himself up completely, yawing and stretching, he saw that Mia's mind was drifting away. Her eyes were clouded with thought, and he couldn't help but wonder what made her crystal blue eyes seem misty. "What's on your mind?" he asked, gently, trying not to startle her.

Mia smiled gently at him. With a small shrug, she answered, "Oh, my parents. I never really knew my mom, but I remember she always called me her 'Little Princess.'" After a moment's hesitation, she added cynically, "Now I know why."

"My dad was never the same after she died. I always guessed that he blamed me for Mom's death, but now... Ben, what is a person supposed to do when her whole world is suddenly turned upside down?" she asked, facing him. "I can't help but wonder what's going to happen to me. This is my world now. The king killed my mom and took away my father's sanity and left me with very little. What can I do? I have magic, but I can't control it and don't know a way to learn how. I can't go home, not after learning this and knowing what I know. He can't get away with something like that!" Anger rolled off her in waves, making Ben cringe beside her.

Warily, Ben watched as a tear formed in the corner of Mia's eye. After a moment or two, she had calmed down enough for him to come up with something to say. "When my dad died, I had to keep busy to stop myself from thinking about it. Maybe it'll help you, too. Besides," he added optimistically, "it wasn't your fault then, and it isn't now." Patting her on the shoulder, then standing, he smiled. "But it will be your fault if we miss breakfast, so c'mon!" And he helped her to her feet.

Mia laughed. "Look who's in such a rush *now*!" she exclaimed. "Thanks, sleepyhead," she murmured. "Let's go."

The second they stepped out of the side chamber, they were doomed. In vain, the pair of them wound through the mountain, trying to follow Trin's directions, but they only succeeded in getting themselves lost. The directions lay forgotten at the back of their minds from the night before.

As they walked through the perfectly chiseled side of the tunnel, Ben ran a hand along the wall. "Imagine who must have made this, probably really good miners. Now this is just an abandoned shaft." He seemed excited by the prospect, and Mia laughed.

"Or it could be the first magician that escaped into the mountains and made this his new home so that he and his family could be safe." She nudged him light-heartedly in the side as he frowned at her.

"How long do you figure it'll take us to get to the central chamber?"

"Obviously, Wizard and Trin are already there. Of course, we don't know how long they were up and Trin knew his way through the passages, so it could take us forever without help," she replied, giggling slightly at Ben's sudden change of subject.

However long Trin and Wizard had been up, they must have assumed that Ben and Mia would be all right and could find their own way. Unfortunately, the opposite was true.

*   *   *   *

"Ben? Ben, where'd you go?" She'd lost him. She had no clue how they'd gotten separated, just that it had happened. Retracing her steps, she heard Ben calling her name. Heading toward the source of the sound, she found him again, and they both breathed a sigh of relief.

"Let's not do that again," Ben muttered, looking around at the walls of the tunnel suspiciously.

Mia nodded and slipped her hand into his. "I agree; hold tight and hopefully that won't happen again." She turned and started to lead the way down the tunnel, not seeing Ben's face starting to glow red in the dim light from the world outside the mountain that had managed to penetrate so deep.

They started to notice that the walls were covered in designs. Some of them were smudged, and no amount of squinting and turning one's head could decipher the picture that was once there. Others were clearer, and they saw that the more legible ones repeated often as they found their way.

Eventually, Ben and Mia found the central chamber where Wizard and Trin were happily in deep conversation, while Katie sat apart from them with an extremely bored expression permanently imprinted on her face, or so it seemed. As soon as she caught sight of the teenagers, she brightened and stood to skip happily over to them.

Shooting a deliberate glance in the direction of Ben's hand holding Mia's, she started talked in her accelerated tone about how dull it was listening to 'Wiz' and Trin.

Ben dropped Mia's hand quickly and went to sit down next to Trin. Grabbing breakfast, Ben started munching before any questions could be directed at him. However, he was careful that he didn't choke as he wolfed it down this time, lest he incite another comment from Mia.

Mia chuckled, but didn't say anything about it. Sitting beside Wizard, she felt eyes probing the top of her ducked head. Looking up, she found Trin staring straight at her. He continued to watch her, even when she met his eye, and she started to squirm under his gaze.

Trin smiled and shook his head as he looked at her. "I apologize, Your Highness, for staring, but as I said before, you look so like your mother." His tone was almost mockingly serious as he addressed her with a slight bow in her direction. Wizard turned to him, alarmed. Obviously, she hadn't gotten around to sharing that information yet.

Putting the pieces together, Mia gasped as her mouth popped open in surprise. "You-- you knew! You knew that I was the Princess! But, how could you when I didn't even know myself?" she babbled.

Katie laughed at her rapid speech. "And you guys say that I talk too fast."

"You do," Ben hushed her. Katie pouted as he swallowed the remainder of the food in his mouth, listened to the conversation intently.

Trin smiled sadly. "I knew your mother very well. There was no possible way that you weren't her child." At the hungry look of Mia's face her continued. "I grew up with Diane; she was my older sister." He looked down carefully at the remains of the dying fire, avoiding Mia's eyes.

Stunned, Mia inspected Trin more closely. He had firelight glinting in the same blue eyes that she and her mother had, same cheekbones, same hair color, and same tall, thinness that made the woman so willowy. While Trin looked more solid than his sister or niece, he looked up and faced her reassuringly as she whispered into the small cave, "Why didn't you tell me before?"

Trin let out a sharp bark of laughter. "What would you

have said? I've been hiding from King Dimitri for all this time. With you going to face him, I wasn't going to let you know where your uncle was in case things turned nasty. They sometimes do with Dimitri," he added darkly. "If he mentioned me to you at all, you would have thought of me instantly and may have accidently done something to let him know. *Involuntarily,* of course," he added, noticing her outraged expression. "I would never assume you would sell me out; you are your mother's daughter. I see her in nearly everything that you do.

Mia frowned but nodded; she couldn't reveal what she didn't know. "I suppose that makes sense. Then, why didn't you stop us from going to the king if you knew how awful he was?" she questioned. There were so many questions to ask Trin, her one connection to her mother, but she knew that some more important than others.

"Would you have listened? I would have loved to tell you and keep you here, but you were on your way to see him. In addition, Ben already didn't trust me. I was worried that if I tried to stop you, you would never have trusted me again. I thought that I was the only one who knew your true identity, and I needed you to come back so that I could help prepare you for the king coming after you." Trin shook his head. "Remember, I refused to come with you? That was because I would have been immediately recognized by King Dimitri and probably sentenced to death. That's why I won't come out of the mountains until you sit on the throne."

Mia's brain was reeling: An uncle who thought she should be the ruler of a world she hadn't even known about a few months ago. "I'm not sure I can do it," she said quietly, her fear creeping out.

"Oh, you won't have to overthrow the king and rule all on your own. The rest of us are here for you," Wizard pitched in, gesturing to the motley crew sitting around the chamber. Besides, we have all the time we need to get you as ready as you have to be. We're here for you now and will be there for you when the time comes."

"Thanks," Mia whispered gratefully. "I guess I need all the help I can get."

It was quiet for a while as everyone contemplated what they could do to help in the coup.

After some time, Trin nodded slowly; then pushing himself up, he pulled the others to their feet. "Come on, I'll show you around the mountains so that you don't get lost." He proceeded to show them how to find their way out of the mountains by using the designs that Ben and Mia had noticed on the walls earlier. The lesson was also to ensure that they didn't get lost while coming in again.

Once outside, he told them that the mountains were always changing and that they would have to get a good feel for where things were without using the mountains as landmarks. He showed them that the outside of their mountain held a scratched symbol on it from Trin's knife. For hours they wandered around, slowly becoming more inclined to leisurely wandering than studious learning. They *tried* to take in everything that the mountains had to teach, but knowing that it would look completely different in the morning wasn't a strong incentive. At the end of the day's lesson, Trin explained that it took him a long time to learn the routes because, at first, he didn't know that the mountains moved.

"Plus," he added, "I found that the mountains covered different parts of the old, unused roads that run in nearly every direction. The roads can take you anywhere except toward Amaria."

At this point, Mia leaned toward Ben and shot him a

quizzical look. "Amaria?" she questioned.

Ben leaned toward her and, as if sharing a secret with her quietly out of the side of his mouth, muttered, "A city on the far northwestern edge of Iceworld."

Mia nodded and went back to listening to Trin.

Before they returned to the cave, the whole group knew the underlying route around their area of the mountains, right down to the hot springs not far from their cave. After they had eaten, Trin sat back to examine Ben and Mia.

"Why don't you go and give Nomis a little exercise?" he suggested. I'm sure that after a few days of flying no more than a mile in each direction, he's ready to get moving around again."

Ben grinned and looked over at Mia, who smiled back and stood up. They raced their way out of the cave and climbed onto Nomis. The dragon lifted off with the usual, comforting rush of air. Soaring through the air around the mountain peaks, Mia calmly rested her chin on Ben's shoulder, her cheek against his ear and shoulders against his back. "I love this," she whispered, sending secret shivers down his back.

Smiling to himself, Ben cleared his throat slightly and shrugged. Mia let him re-adjust and then replaced her chin. Wanting to say something, Ben thought of a conversation topic that he wanted to surprise her with. "Mia, did you know that Katie's part Golen?" he asked lightly, hoping for a bigger reaction than his tone warranted.

Mia turned her head to look at him, her face suddenly even more alarmingly close. "Part *what*?"

Ben felt like he should smack himself on the forehead: he kept forgetting that Mia wasn't raised in Iceworld like he was and didn't know all the things he did about the world.

"Golens are small seers; they see the future. Whatever they predict always comes true, particularly not the way you would have expected. There's no way you can try to prevent it from happening," he informed her, a grim smile on his face.

Mia nodded slowly. "All right." There was a slight pause as she grasped what this meant. "So what did Katie predict that came true?" she questioned. "She never said anything prophetic."

"Since she's part Ice Elf, I think she does prophetic ice sculptures. Ben swallowed hard before continuing. "Well, there was that one sculpture that she did of us, back when we were arguing over whether or not you'd done magic, you remember?" Mia nodded. That one came true."

There was a moment while Mia pulled the memory from the deep recesses of her mind. When she remembered what he was talking about, she nodded. "But... when did that happen?" she asked, not remembering ever sitting in front of Ben while they were on Nomis. "Why don't I remember it?"

"You were asleep," Ben explained. "It was right after you made that light, and we were leaving the mountains. You had passed out, and I pulled you up in front of me on Nomis, just like Katie sculpted. I woke you up once we landed. I found out then about Katie."

Mia simply sighed and replied in an off-put voice, "Okay." She remained silent for a painstaking moment before speaking again. "Ben, what if I can't beat him? The king, I mean. What if I can't learn the magic that I need fast enough?" She was gloomy and insecure, and Ben knew it.

Ben thought over her words for a moment. He could hear the fear lacing Mia's voice, and he didn't blame her but didn't know what he could say to make her feel better. Then something Wizard had said occurred to him. "You will learn everything you need and more. I'll bet that you'll learn enough to make you even more powerful than King Dimitri," he told her firmly, laughter lining his voice.

Mia caught on the humorous edge and couldn't help. "Well, thanks, Ben! The king should be afraid of me!" she exclaimed, biting back a bubble of laughter.

Ben laughed loudly, making light of the joke. "But of course! He'll drop to his knees and beg for your forgiveness: 'Please, don't use your awesome power!'" Both of them were helpless with laughter.

When the final giggles and chuckles subsided, they turned Nomis around and headed back towards the cave. Upon entering, they found Wizard kneeling on the ground with Katie, Trin watching over them, working on something in the tunnel.

Looking up, Wizard spotted them first. "Good, you two are back! Mia, come and place your hand here," she instructed. She stood and brushed of the front of her robes, stepping out of Mia's way.

Mia walked over, noticing that there was a block of ice filling the doorway to one of the many smaller caves that they had passed that morning. There was a smaller chunk on the wall next to the block, the same shape of the hand plate in Tancredo. "What will happen?" she asked suspiciously. She remembered the alarm that had gone off in Tancredo and wanted to avoid that situation a second time around.

Wizard spared her only an offended glance. "Nothing at all. We've situated our own rooms, and this is so that we each have a bit of privacy. Mia, you'll share a room with Katie. Ben, yours is the next on the left," she pointed him down the tunnel.

Ben walked across the passage and down about fifteen feet to an identical slab of ice set over the opening of a small cavern. Skeptically, he pressed the palm of his hand against the small tablet beside the "door." The door slid away, letting him in without resistance. Turning away from it, he heard it slide shut as he returned to the others; he saw that they had worked the door so that it would let both Mia and Katie in. There were two tablets, one at a more reasonable height for the elf.

Trin clapped his hands together. "Well, I think we're all set. We should all get some rest: we have a big day ahead of us," he added, yawning slightly.

Katie nodded vigorously, a huge yawn stretching her mouth. "I'm r-r-r-really tired," she informed them, mid-yawn, settling the matter. Soon all had fallen very soundly asleep.

Chapter 17: Magic Class

Mia sat up, suddenly awake for the first time in her new room. Since she knew from past experience that Katie whistled in her sleep, she wasn't surprised by the high-pitched noise filling the air. Smiling, the girl stood up. "Come on, Katie, wake up." She prodded and picked up the bleary-eyed elf and started towards the main chamber through the twisting passage ways. The others, Ben, Trin, and Wizard, were already there, waiting for her. Ben looked as if he, too, had just woken up.

"Tired, Ben?" Mia asked, laughing, sitting beside him and grinning. He gave her a look of such annoyance that she couldn't help but laugh harder. "Sorry, I asked," she joked.

Mia found herself dreaming of the hot springs that Trin had shown them the day before. The warm water bubbled and ran out a break in the side of the rocky pool. It then flowed down to a large river that eventually led to the sea.

Ben informed Mia about the people who were lost at sea and never heard from again. No one knew whether it was because they had reached land and didn't or couldn't write, because they kept sailing and ran out of food, or because they simply sailed off the edge of the world all together. Mia thought the story was interesting but didn't think much of it.

Mia felt horrible with an unwanted layer of grime covering every inch of her skin, so she excused herself, left for the springs, and wished the whole way that she had raspberry soap and a large, fluffy towel to dry off with.

When she reached the spring, Mia undressed and quickly hopped into the water to avoid the chilling wind that blew through the mountains. She felt the warmth pleasantly close in around her shivering body. Relaxing, Mia submerged herself in the water, her hair soaking and floating around her head in a cloud of black. She surfaced and floated on her back, not opening her eyes just yet, but enjoying the peace and heat of the springs. She was still imagining the soap: round, pink, raspberry- scented.

Mia swam across the wide pool and leaned against the hard rock. Wiping the water out of her face, she blinked open her eyes. What she saw, she couldn't believe.

On the ledge of the rock, there sat a little blob of color. Mia couldn't make it out through the water that was dripping into her eyes from her wet hair. Once again she wiped her eyes and looked at the pink blob more closely.

No... could it? Yes, it is! She reached out and seized the small object. It was waxy, and once her wet fingers closed over it, it became slippery and harder to hold than at first. It was the soap she had longed and hoped for.

Smiling happily, Mia scrubbed herself down as thoroughly as she could. Even her hair was subjected to the scented soap. When she finished washing, she watched her suds flow gently down the creek and knew it would eventually make it to the ocean. Content to just float for a moment or two, she smiled and then stood, wiping water from her eyes and face. She was tired, which didn't surprise her. Swimming and a long, hot bath always made her exhausted.

When she stepped out of the water, Mia could feel that the old layer of dead skin and dirt had been washed off. The cool air refreshed her, and she beamed with happiness. The glum and dreadful feelings of facing her mother's murderer had been washed away with the grime and soapy water. Shivering, she looked around for her clothes and spotted the yearned for large, fluffy towel. Drying herself quickly, Mia sagged with relief that she didn't have to wear her clothes while soaking wet. Completely drying off, she located her clothing, got dressed, and headed back to the cave.

Ben was in the main cave talking to Trin about how he should go to the town and see what was happening when he smelled a sweet, tangy, yet unusual smell. He looked around, taking in the scent, widening his nostrils just to breathe it deeper. It was so good; he never wanted it to fade. Looking around for the source, Ben saw Mia entering the cavern and stared at her, dumbstruck.

"That smell is coming from you?" he asked, surprised. He wasn't aware of anything in Iceworld that smelled like that.

"Yeah, why? Don't you like it?" Mia asked, suddenly feeling very self-conscious. She picked up a lock of her hair to smell; it smelled perfectly all right to her. She looked around at the other three that made up the group. "You guys like it, don't you?"

Trin nodded. "It's nice, sweet, tart, bouncy, and very fresh. It's very much like you, Mia. Though I admit, I've never smelled it before." He took in the sweet smell and exhaled slowly. "Yes, it's very nice indeed. What is it?"

"Raspberry, it's a small, red fruit that grows in the...spring..." she trailed off, realizing that only Ben, to whom she had explained it, would know what she was talking about. "He doesn't even like it," she threw in, trying to cover her awkward moment, pointing at Ben.

Ben, looking somewhat shocked by Mia's accusation, opened his mouth to protest, but nothing came out. Finally, when he managed to get his tongue and voice to work, he replied, "It smells great; you just surprised me." He hoped he didn't sound as stupid as he felt.

Mia laughed. "Thank you, Ben." She sat down and held her towel in her arms. "You know, I got the soap and this towel in a really unusual way... I had been wishing for it, and when I was bathing, there it was! It was great!"

Katie scrambled up to sit on Mia's lap. "I love it. It smells great, really pretty." She smiled up at the girl and wiggled her toes. She looked over at Wizard, who had remained silent and solemn. "What's wrong, Wiz?"

Wizard considered not saying anything for a while, but then decided it would be better to say what she knew and then replied, "Mia, you used magic, a kind of summoning magic. It was dangerous because you didn't know you were doing it. Do you feel tired at all?"

Mia nodded. "A little, but it's not horrible. I always feel a little tired whenever I have a hot bath."

"That tiredness comes from you drawing on your reserve of energy to use magic. Even though it's probably within your limits, please don't think about something with that kind of concentration until you've learned a little bit more. You could drain all of your energy without even knowing it."

Mia nodded, agreeing. "All right. Whatever you say…"

Ben rolled his eyes. "Figures that Mia would be the one that would die for a good bath." He chuckled and got Mia's elbow in his side for his trouble.

Wizard watched the two of them, smiling, before she turned specifically back to Mia. "So, are you as ready to begin your training as you seem?" When Mia nodded, Wizard smiled grimly. "Good. Magic can be strenuous work until one is accustomed to working with it on a daily basis. When you're ready, I'll be waiting outside for you."

Mia put her towel and soap in her room and hurried after Wizard, who was waiting at the mouth of the cave. Mia stepped into the cool mountain air, kicking a rock as she did so.

Wizard turned around in slight surprise. "That was much quicker than I was expecting. Find your way all right?"

Mia nodded. "Yeah, I think I'm getting better." She anxiously ran her fingers through her hair and forced herself to take a deep breath. "So, what am I going to learn?" She hated not knowing when her power was going to show up. It was a part of herself that she had no control over, and she was ready to gain it.

Wizard pondered over her pupil's question. "We are going to start with basics. Learning to focus your energy to the best of your ability and testing your limits are going to be the two main things for a while. "

Mia looked at her curiously. "Limits? What do you mean by that? You brought those up in the cave too, talking about the soap and towel."

Wizard thought as she came up with a way to word her answer. "Well, a magician, sorcerer, or sorceress can only use so much power because it relies heavily on the magic user's energy. If he or she uses too much, it drains his or her life away." Wizard glanced at Mia, whose confused expression spoke volumes of how she comprehended a piece of information like that.

Seeking for an explanation, Wizard started, "If you overexert yourself while running, you might keel over, right?" Mia nodded, unsure where the conversation was leading. "Right. Well, it's pretty much the same with magic. Overdo it, and you might as well stand still and let your opponent to kill you."

Mia's eyes widened. "Oh, that's comforting," she said sarcastically.

Shrugging, Wizard went on. "I wouldn't worry about it if I were you. Strength comes with practice. By the time you'll have to face King Dimitri, you'll be much better and harder to beat." She smiled encouragingly.

Mia nodded slowly, contemplating Wizard's words. "So, how are you going to test my 'limits' without killing me?" She looked up carefully at her mentor.

Wizard chuckled grimly, her lips forming a tight line. "Yes, I thought you would bring that up. I'll only push you until you get a little tired. By then I should have a good idea of your limits." She stepped away from the mountains, striding purposefully forward. Turning sharply, Wizard hashed out a quick order. "Create a block of ice."

Mia frowned and concentrated. In a few seconds, she had a chunk of ice that would be more appropriate to call a cube than a block. Its diminutive size shocked Wizard, for she had heard about the things this girl was capable of.

"You have to really want it," the older woman advised. "You have to feel as if your life depends on making a block of ice that's exactly the same as size as you are."

Mia, inspired by Wizard's words, smiled and closed her eyes. She started muttering, forming what was going on inside her head into words. In a moment, she stood, completely winded and out of breath, staring at a perfect ice sculpture of herself. She grinned, panting, and managed to point out, "It even has my exact shoe size." She laughed wheezily and sunk down to sit on the cold earth.

Wizard chuckled at Mia's cheekiness but frowned. "You'll have to learn discipline if you want to learn what I want to teach you." She inspected the ice-replica of her pupil and grinned a little wider. "Though, that was incredibly clever."

Mia nodded and agreed to follow Wizard's order to the letter. When she stood, she heard the *shh-shh* of footsteps coming from the tunnel.

The sound came from Trin and Ben as they walked out of the cave. Katie was on the older man's shoulder. "We're going to go hunting," Trin told the two women. He took Katie off of his shoulder gently and deposited her near Mia on a small, rocky ledge before leading a very interested Ben away into the mountains.

Katie watched them go, a look of sheer boredom on her face. "I didn't want to go with them. I'd rather watch you learn magic," she told Mia. Perking up, the elf plopped herself into a sitting position and folded her tiny hands in her lap. "What have you gotten to so far?" she asked Wizard.

Wizard recounted what they had done and responded, "We've covered blocks, or sculptures, of ice and are about to see if she can create and sustain a small snowstorm."

Already feeling a little tired, Mia nodded grimly. "All right. Let's get started."

Wizard moved around and positioned Mia in a way that would help her balance and be able to control her wind and snow a little easier. Soon large, fluffy white flakes were falling on their heads, and Katie had to stand to shake herself off.

Katie watched and sometimes argued about Mia's magic lessons. She would give her opinion about things or point out how she believed that Wizard was wrong, which started an argument between the two. Occasionally, the elf would try to teach Mia a new thing or two, but more often than not, Wizard put her foot down. The magician didn't seem to like the four inch-tall Ice Elf taking over her magic lesson.

As Mia was trying out one of her assignments, Wizard and Katie stood by, arguing still. She started to sway on her feet and her eyes drooped, but she pressed on, wanting to please her teacher. A mild wind picked up, at first giving them a refreshing cool burst of air sweeping through the mountains.

As the wind's speed and ferocity slowly increased, Wizard silenced Katie with a hand and turned in horror to see Mia attempting the latest spell with no supervision. Cursing herself, Wizard ran forward and shook Mia out of her torpor.

Coming back to her senses a little, Mia stared at Wizard with a blank, bewildered expression that couldn't be expressed in words due to the heaviness of her tongue.

"Mia, listen to me. If wind starts blowing with an unsettling suddenness, stop the spell you are trying. It means that the spell could very well push you too far, sometimes only to unconsciousness. If the spell is large enough, it will drain all of your energy and life away immediately, and you'll have nothing left." She guided Mia back towards the mouth of the cavern. "It's time you got some food and then rest."

Just then, Trin and Ben returned, carrying a couple of bundles that were wrapped tightly in animal hide. Wizard looked at them warily. "What are those?" she asked in a reluctant tone of voice.

"Rabbits," Ben replied happily. "We found them, and Trin taught me how to catch and kill them. He even showed me how to ski-"

"Urgh, I don't want to hear about it! Just come inside and cook it!" Wizard grumbled, disgusted.

Ben grinned and handed Trin his bundle. Following them to the main cavern and sitting down, he sighed contentedly. "You know, it was a lot of fun. Trin showed me all sorts of tricks, like how to build snares, tie different kinds of knots. We even got on Nomis and flew around for a while. I hope we can do the same kind of thing tomorrow," he said, speaking rapidly enough to challenge Katie.

Trin shook his head and smiled, setting up the pan for the meat and carefully lighting the fire. He eyed Mia, who was dozing off against the far wall.

Mia had leaned back during Ben's fast chatter, right against the hard rock behind her. She was so tired that even the unshifting wall was comfortable. Hearing what was going on wasn't a problem, but keeping her eyes open took more effort than Mia wanted to think about.

Wizard saw Trin's gaze and followed it to her young pupil. Alarmed, she felt incredibly guilty. *I shouldn't have let her go on for that long. I'll have to be more careful about how hard I push her in lessons from now on, at least until she's stronger.*

Mia sat back and yawned. "I'm really tired. I-- I think I-- I'll go to bed." She got up and started wobbling towards the door.

Trin looked at Ben with an amused look in his eye. "Ben, why don't you help Mia to her room while we're preparing dinner? We don't want her to fall over, not without someone to catch her." Trin's wide smile mocked the younger man.

Ben narrowed his eyes and glared at Trin suspiciously, wondering how much the old mountain man knew. Getting up, he crossed over to Mia, wrapped an arm around her waist delicately and led her along the tunnel to her room. Once she was settled and asleep in her room, Ben hurried back to the main cavern. "Why on earth did you do that?" he growled at them before sitting down angrily.

"You are in love with her," Wizard stated, putting some of the cooked rabbit on her plate. He looked like he would protest but thought better of it because of the look on her face.

Ben scowled at her. "Okay, then does everyone know?"

"Yes," the loud reply came from all three parts of the remaining group.

Considering this, Ben's face adopted a rather sick expression. "Does *Mia* know?"

Wizard chuckled. "She's the only one you seem to make an effort to hide it from. For the rest of us, it's extremely easy to spot." Katie giggled quietly.

"Ben, I wouldn't be that surprised if Mia *did* know. She's so much like her mother," Trin explained. "When Mia's dad, Simon, met Diane, he fell in love with her immediately. Diane knew it almost as soon as he did. Eventually, she came to love him just as much in return, but never said anything because of all the romantic notions she had in her head. It wasn't until she was told that she had to marry the chosen suitor that she ever admitted to anything. He never had the guts to say anything until he heard that Diane was arguing with our parents about how she wanted to marry him."

Ben absorbed this information before abruptly changing the subject. "So, are we just going to hang around in the mountains until the king decides he's going to come in after us?"

Trin shrugged, his face growing grimmer as he returned to the present after his reminiscing. It seemed like a cruel reality for him. "I have no clue what we can do, Ben. The best thing right now is to wait." With that he stood and left for his room, the others departing shortly afterward.

Chapter 18: Hiding

For the next four and a half months, Trin knew happiness again. The months passed seamlessly; he had human company that wasn't forced. It was nice to speak to someone whom he knew would speak back to him. He was tired of solitude. He realized over time that his niece was a more cautious version of her mother, and he couldn't help smiling around her. Before she and the others had come, Trin had spent many lonely years in the mountains, praying that someone new would take the throne.

The mountain man taught Ben about surviving in the mountains, such as how to hunt for different kinds of animals. They also worked out how to teach Nomis new maneuvers while in the air. That way, if needed, the large dragon could dodge and evade arrows shot at them without throwing his riders off.

Mia continued to learn magic from Wizard. Sometimes Trin would stop by before taking Ben out and tell her things that Diane had done magically. Mia would try some of her mother's feats and tell her uncle how they worked out. Other times, Trin was her only teacher, and Wizard went with Ben to see if there could be anything done to further his education. Katie was always present at Mia's lessons: she didn't like watching animals being killed and flying circles in midair even less. Katie was almost always bouncing from place to place, asking questions and being in the center of things. She was often told to sit still and let Mia concentrate, which was easier than expected for the little ball of energy.

Mia's natural abilities grew, and she could handle larger and more complicated tasks. Winter Magic was simple; it was the thing that Mia could do without thinking about, as she had done when she had lost her necklace. She went from never knowing when or where her magic was going to kick in to being able to control every aspect of it imaginable. The magic wouldn't happen unless she called it or if it was a natural reaction. Unlike a knee-jerk reaction, which was involuntary, magic was apparently a reflex that could be developed. Eventually, her eighteenth birthday passed, and, as happy as she was, it didn't seem as important as it normally would have.

Wizard was thinking lately about how much better life was in the mountains than in the castle. King Dimitri was cruel, cold, mean-hearted, and threatening. Instead, she was spending her time in the company of a small group that was usually happy, except for the glum prospect of the inevitable battle between Mia and the king. No one enjoyed thinking about that subject, so they avoided conversing about it. Things were still better than being locked into the dungeon because she had been the unlucky bearer of bad news one too many times.

Sometimes, someone would find a stray wanderer walking dazedly through the mountains. Either Wizard or Mia helped to escort them out and then erased the memory of how they had left the mountains. That way, there was no one to say that they had seen Mia or the others to anybody who may be looking for them.

Ben walked through his days trying to shut out the delicious smell of raspberries that seemed to follow him everywhere he went. Even in his sleep, he dreamed of the scent and the person wearing it. He longed to tell Mia how he felt but was nervous. Perhaps she didn't have the same feelings for him, and then he would just wind up making a fool of himself while having to share a mountain and every meal with her.

Fortunately enough, he didn't see much of her during the day. Ever since Trin had run out of things to teach him, Ben had started going into town to keep an eye on the "Wanted" signs. They were never taken down but were commonly ignored by the townspeople.

One day, when Ben came back, he sat down and told them that a new poster was put up beside the "Wanted" one. It announced King Dimitri's Masque Ball. "It takes place in two months. It says he's inviting everyone from all over Iceworld. The two months, I suppose, is to give people from far away time to prepare." He shook his head, seeming agitated. "That's going to be a lot of people. I hope the palace has a huge ballroom."

Trin nodded. "Oh yes, the ballroom was designed to hold many, many people," he said. "I remember going in there with Diane and playing tag. It's in a circular shape so there aren't any corners that you could get trapped in. It was quite fun."

"The king hasn't used it for anything so far, but every king has to have a ball sooner or later, for he has to choose a wife, get married, and produce heirs for his line to go on. It's the law of the royals," Wizard said glumly. "We have to get into that ball and stop him then. If he chooses a bride, gets married and has children, Mia, you won't be the *Ice Princess* anymore. You're just going to be a girl who used to be."

Ben growled under his breath. Changing the subject slightly, he asked, "So how do you think she'll get in? Do you expect the guards to let Mia in as if she were a guest? In case you've forgotten, she's one of the most wanted people in Iceworld. There's a price on her head. It's too dangerous."

"Is not, Ben!" Mia protested. "I've been training for this for months. I have a better shot now than ever. It might be too late if we wait any longer." Her stubborn face made Ben nod in reluctant agreement.

"Fine, but you'll still have a hard time getting in," he pointed out, trying to be the reasonable one. He did *not* want Mia going into that castle alone again.

"Well, Ben's right," Trin said slowly and thoughtfully. "They'll never let the Outlaw Princess in, but they *will* let a lovely, masked young woman in with her escort." A mischievous grin stole over his expression. Everyone turned their heads as one to look at Ben.

Ben, knowing what they were getting at, shook his head. "Oh no, no way! I am not going to any balls. Besides, I can't even dance!"

Chapter 19: Dance Class

"C'mon, Ben, step up. You need to learn if you're going to the king's ball!" Trin chuckled as he spoke to the younger man.

Ben grumbled and got up. *I shouldn't have let them talk me into this*, he thought. He glanced at Mia, who was watching him and laughing, and scowled. "It's not that funny."

"Yes, it is. You should see your face," she replied, giggling. She smiled. "C'mon, Ben, it won't kill you to dance with me." She held out her hand, waiting for him to step forward.

"How do you know? I might be allergic to raspberries," Ben replied quickly, staying where he was.

"Oh, you big baby! If you were allergic, you'd be dead by now. " Mia rolled her eyes dramatically at him. "I sit next to you all the time!"

"Ben, just get up there," Trin said, pushing the young man forward. Ben tripped toward Mia, managing not to fall. Wizard and Katie held back their laughter; Mia laughed openly.

"C'mon! What's the problem?" she asked Ben through her laughter.

Ben shuffled his feet against the ground and mumbled, "I can't dance." Quite the opposite of what he'd been expecting, nobody laughed any harder at this information.

Wizard spoke up, nodding. "Well, that's why you're learning, isn't it?" She chuckled, and then both she and Katie burst out with pent up laughter.

Ben glared at them. Mia saw the look and calmed herself enough to stop laughing. "It's all right, Ben. I don't know how to dance all that much either, but I'm at least willing to learn. Unlike somebody…" She raised an eyebrow in his direction.

"Yeah, well, this is probably worse for me than you," Ben retorted, but he stepped up and loosely, awkwardly, put his hands around her waist.

"It won't be as bad as all that," Trin reprimanded, stepping closer to the couple in order to position their hands. One of Mia's went on Ben's shoulder, the other in the air, while Ben's hands went more tightly around Mia's waist and into her suspended hand. "There, keep your hands in those positions the whole time. The key is practice. Ben, slide forward on the balls of your feet. Mia, pay attention and feel which way he's stepping and react with a mirrored action," Trin instructed. Ben followed his order and slid his right foot toward Mia. She was pushed ever so slightly backward and was forced to slide her left foot backward.

Nodding, Trin directed them to dance in a small circle, alternating feet and keeping time. Wizard created simple music with a steady tempo for them. Occasionally, Trin would correct an error, showing them what they were doing wrong, how to do it right, and then made them dance through it again.

Ben felt slightly humiliated by the whole thing, but as time went on, their movements became less awkward. He became more and more comfortable with his arms around Mia, even began to enjoy it.

On the other hand, Mia was having fun. She made a joke out of it when she messed up and laughed about it with her friends. Perhaps, she thought, the ball wouldn't be a complete waste if she got to dance for most of the night.

Wizard and Katie completely abandoned watching the lesson after a while and started arguing quietly about the couple's "disguises." Katie said that Mia's dress should be blue and white while Wizard argued that it should be deep red. They didn't settle on it, for Trin turned around and shushed them as they got louder.

Every night, after dinner, Trin would put Ben and Mia through several different dances, to make sure they knew more than just one.

Wizard and Katie continued to work out disguises for the Masque Ball so that neither of the teens would be recognized by anyone. Ben wasn't in as much danger as Mia, but it had been pointed out that one of the guards might realize that he had been on the dragon when the Ice Princess was apprehended. Besides, it was a masque ball; anyone without a mask would stick out, except for King Dimitri.

Iceworld

As the day of the ball drew closer, Mia and Ben became more anxious and worried. Katie and Wizard did their best to soothe the couple's nerves while Trin was preparing them for every possibility. When only a couple of weeks were left, Katie and Wizard got the outfits ready and told Mia about them.

Katie herself made a sculpture of what Ben would look like for Mia to see. Nodding slowly and thoughtfully, Mia took it from the little elf.

"Wow, I had no idea that you guys were planning for us to be fully decked out like this," she said quietly, staring down at the figure in her hand with a slight smile on her face.

Katie sighed. "Wiz says that at a royal ball, you'll stick out if you aren't. So, there you are." She waved her hands vaguely at the sculpture.

Mia laughed. "I imagine so. You know, I could see Ben in something like this." A small smile crept onto the corners of her mouth. "I almost feel guilty that he won't see my outfit until the ball," she said, tucking the sculpture away. "C'mon, Katie. Wizard's giving me another lesson today."

Katie grinned and ran after Mia as she walked away. Wizard caught sight of the elf and turned away slightly. The elf had won the argument about Mia's dress color, but then again, Wizard had known she would. Something else entirely popped into her mind as she saw Mia tucking the sculptures away. "Mia, you can't wear your necklace to the palace." Her expression and tone were solemn and apologetic.

One look at Mia's shocked, incredulous face, and she launched into an explanation. "It's the only thing that will be recognized by anybody in the room, especially the king. You already look so much like your mother that it's dangerous for you to even go. On top of that, the king has already met you and could probably recognize you without it."

"No, I understand," Mia murmured, holding the snowflake tightly in her fist, she took a deep breath of the stingingly cold air. "It'll make it less likely for him to immediately recognize me because he'll be expecting me to wear it." Closing her eyes, she hated the thought of leaving it behind. "Can I just take it with me? It doesn't have to be visible…" Her hopeful eyes flew open to see the reluctant face of her mentor. "I'll hide in my dress, in a pocket or something…" She pleaded with Wizard until the older woman complied and agreed to let Mìa take the necklace with her.

Chapter 20: The Transformation

On the night of the ball, Ben and Mia stood by Nomis and waited for Trin and Wizard's parting words. Katie was resting on Wizard's shoulder; the elf wasn't to go with the two to the palace.

Ben looked skeptically at Mia. Though the young woman had learned a lot of magic by now, he wasn't sure how she was going to magically conjure up clothes for them. He felt like he should have a bag of dress clothes so that he could change. Glancing down, he couldn't help but wonder how she was going to change their slightly tattered clothing into outfits for a royal ball.

Mia smiled tightly at him. Her blue coat had lost most of its color, but her cheeks and eyes made up for the loss. Anxiety and adrenaline made her flush and her eyes shine at him. Luckily, both of them had stopped growing and had never needed more clothes.

Trin broke the silence first. "The traditional advice is to be careful and be yourself, but, considering the circumstances, the latter would be bad advice." He smiled, putting a hand on each Ben and Mia's shoulders. Looking them solemnly in the eye, he imparted what advice he was giving. "Try to avoid long conversations about yourselves. Keep your masks on, and no one should recognize you," he told them seriously.

Nodding, Mia turned to Wizard, who had had more experience with the king than the rest of them combined. She looked anxiously at her mentor who seemed nervous and dissatisfied with the situation. Seeing Mia's gaze trained on her, Wizard smiled and stepped forward. "Stay away from the king if you can. He will be going through the crowd though; it's his obligation to dance with all the eligible women." To Ben, she added, "Without her bruise, Mia shouldn't attract too much attention, so you shouldn't have much of a problem either, but keep an eye on her and keep her safe." Her face grew very serious as she embraced the two young adults.

"Good luck, you'll need it," Katie chipped in shortly from Wizard's shoulder.

Ben swallowed nervously and nodded. He clambered onto Nomis, helping Mia up behind him, and nudged the dragon with his knees. "Bye!" he called over the rush of beating wings.

"We'll contact you as soon as we can!" Mia yelled to their three friends as they took off. Nomis quickly sped up to a higher altitude and soared between the mountain peaks. For a few minutes, there was a silence that threatened to stretch all the way to the road. Ben sat in front of Mia, wondering what he could say to keep her from dreading the coming evening. "So when you take over, I'll be able to come into the castle whenever I want, right?"

Mia pulled her chin from its resting place on Ben's shoulder and stared at him, shocked by his confidence. She smiled and chuckled. "No, Ben, I'll never let you in!" she joked sarcastically. She hugged him around his waist and his face flushed.

Laughing, Ben shrugged. "Fine, I'll break in," he retorted. His laughter trailed away, and the silence that followed the brief conversation was more comfortable than the previous one.

Resting her chin on his shoulder again, Mia looked at him thoughtfully. "Ben, do you really think I can do this? Beat the king, I mean," she added, wanting to hear his encouragement. It was his opinion that she gained the most confidence from and wanted reassurance.

There was a hesitation before Ben answered. He looked at her out of the corner of his eye. She was beautifully, yet sadly, hopeful. "Of course you can Mia, and if that 'king' knows what's best for him, he'd better watch his back," he said heatedly. Seeing her expression light up with the praise he was giving her, he continued. "Mia, you'll do fine. Just don't think about it more than you have to. You're the most powerful sorceress I've ever heard of; you won't have a problem defeating him. Besides," he added, smiling again, "you would make a better queen than that oaf makes a king."

Mia smiled wide, hugging him again. "Thanks, Ben." Turning her gaze back to the expanse before them, Mia straightened and pointed ahead. "Look, there's the road!" she exclaimed.

Nodding, Ben nudged Nomis with his knee, signaling him to turn toward the road, where they had planned to leave Nomis and send the dragon back to the mountains for Wizard, Trin, and Katie when it was time. Once they landed, Mia slid off the dragon's hard, scaly back, followed by Ben.

Shooing Nomis so they could travel into the city inconspicuously, Ben turned to face Mia, with an embarrassed expression on his face. "I'll look away, and let you change," he offered, turning to face away from her completely. Mia simply smiled as he did.

"You don't have to, Ben. I'm already dressed," Mia's voice laughed lightly.

Ben turned back, and found Mia's appearance altered greatly. Her black hair was curly and pinned loosely atop her head, with two curling locks of hair that fell into her face. The bridge of her nose was decorated by a black, jeweled mask that hid her face from her cheekbones to her eyebrows, showing her electric blue eyes beneath. Instead of the pants and heavy jacket she had been wearing, the dress she now wore was sky blue, decorated by diamond-like flecks on the very full skirt. Silver, handless gloves covered her forearms, and small, poofy sleeves hung just off her shoulder. The tips of her silver shoes poked through the folds of material. She wore a diamond necklace and earrings.

Ben stared at her, completely awestruck. At that moment, Mia was the most stunning, exquisite being he'd ever seen. His jaw hung open as he gaped at her openly.

In response to Ben's stunned silence, Mia turned pink in the light of the setting sun. Her blush only increased her own prettiness. "Well, say something, Ben. Don't just stand there," she said.

Ben roused himself from his stupor, shaking his head. "That didn't take you very long, did it?" he questioned carefully, trying not to show how flustered he was.

Mia laughed, relaxing a little. "There's not a compliment in you, is there?" Shrugging, she looked Ben up and down; trying to focus on the small sculpture Katie had made her. "It's your turn now." She grinned, a sparkle glinting in her eye.

Seeing the look in her eye, Ben took a step backwards, hands in front of him, warding off anything that Mia might think of doing to him for not commenting on how pretty she was. "What are you going to do, Mia?"

Throwing him an exasperated, incredulous look, Mia shook her head disbelievingly. "Nothing big, now come here! It's easier when you're closer," she ordered him sternly. Ben took a few tentative steps closer. "I'm only altering your appearance, after all." She waved a hand through the air, dismissing the fact as if it were only a trifling matter.

Ben nodded. "Okay, but can you tell me what you're dressing me up in *before* you work your magic?"

Mia chuckled. "Too late, Ben, look." She pointed to his clothing, which had become a black tuxedo.

Ben looked down at it. Ben's mouth dropped open in shock for just a moment. The tuxedo was completely black, down to the tie. The only things that weren't the high polished looking ebony were his starch white shirt and sky blue vest. Mia smiled at her handiwork and handed him a mask. It was black and much more masculine than the fashionable one Mia had on.

Sliding in onto his face, Ben regretted he'd let Mia see his shocked admiration, he grumbled, "Show off," in her direction, making her laugh.

Clapping her hands together enthusiastically, Mia smiled and twirled, making her skirt fan out around her. "That was nothing! First, let me clear away Nomis's tracks, and then you can see my greatest trick yet!" she said, her tone bubbly. Waving a hand at the deep holes in the snow where Nomis had stood, she filled them up with snow. It soon looked as if they had never been there. Satisfied, Mia turned to face the road once more.

Ben watched anxiously as she closed her eyes and bowed her head, obviously focusing. He didn't want to disturb her and so stood watching silently.

For a moment, Mia continued to concentrate. Soon, there was a bright, shining mass sitting directly on the road's path. It dulled to a shimmering, and soon the shimmering had ceased, and it took on shape.

A large box appeared, suspended in the air by four circles. In the front of the box, a lip curled out and two long poles extended from next to the circles, which grew spokes. In between the poles, two large creatures appeared, each owning four legs. On the lip, a figure started to materialize. The box became more elaborate, with intricately designed patterns.

Soon, a lavish white carriage with two white horses stood ready to pull them down the road. From the driver's seat sprung a man dressed in white.

Ben reeled back as he caught sight of the driver's face. The only trace of color on his entire face was the black of his pupils, for everything else was drained of all color. Mia shuddered and moved forward to stand next to him, tapping him on the shoulder as she did so, and the driver opened the door and politely smiled at them, waiting for them to get in the carriage so he that could take them to the ball.

From the moment his hand touched the handle of the carriage door, color started flooding into him. His hair darkened to blonde, his eyes grew to a deep gray color, and cheeks acquired a ruddy color as the rest of his skin tinged faintly pink in the cold. At least he no longer looked like the snow surrounding them. Satisfied, Mia nodded and climbed into the carriage.

Clambering in after Mia, Ben glanced nervously at her from beside her. She was slumped over slightly in her seat, and her eyes had a groggy haze over them. "Mia, are you all right?" he asked cautiously. "You overworked yourself, didn't you?"

Mia nodded sluggishly. "Yeah. Next time, I'm leaving the driver in his own creepy version. That drained too much of my energy. I'll have to rest on the way to the palace," she said sleepily, her head starting to droop.

Ben shook his head. "I don't mind. Come here; you'll fall over if you stay there," he told her, tugging her closer to his own seat. She came easily, but her head lolled onto his shoulder listlessly: Mia was already asleep. Gently, he raised his hand to brush a lock of hair out of her face. He hesitated and then pushed the soft, black strands behind her ear.

Putting his arm around her waist, Ben waited out the unusually smooth ride to the palace. Usually a carriage would skid across the icy road. Wondering if Mia had done anything to the carriage to make it more stable, Ben looked out the window to the best of his ability without shifting Mia from her apparently comfortable position.

Part of him worried that she wouldn't be awake enough at the ball and would suffer some mistake, blowing their cover. The larger part of him, however, wasn't worried because once she woke up, she would be too nervous to think of sleeping.

When they finally pulled up to the palace wall, the carriage rolled smoothly through the gates. The driver allowed the horses to prance lightly around the drive to the steps leading to the main doors. When the carriage came to a halt, the driver bounced out of his seat to the ground. Opening the door, he waited for the pair to step out.

Ben gently shook Mia's shoulder to wake her. Mia opened her eyes blearily and looked at him. "We're there already?" She straightened up, adjusting her hair self-consciously, yawning.

Ben nodded sympathetically. "Yep, come on," he said, stepping out. He held out his hand to help Mia. Her slender, gloved hand appeared, landing perfectly in his. She ducked under the low door and stepped down. As soon as she shifted her weight to the foot on the step, her ankle weakened, her balance failed, and she fell.

Reacting quickly, Ben grabbed her around the waist tightly, keeping her from falling farther. This maneuver brought Mia's face alarmingly close to his, and he was overwhelmed by the smell of raspberries coming off her skin. He was so shocked that he couldn't think to do anything but stare into her eyes. Mia's face quickly flushed red, and Ben was sure his was doing the same.

Mia, still blushing, looked down past their shoulders. "Sorry, Ben." A small smile crept onto her lips. "I guess the ride wasn't as long as it needed to be. I still don't have my feet very firmly on the ground." Pausing, she looked at their feet and added gently, "And I mean that literally."

Ben glanced down and saw that Mia's feet were dangling a few inches above the ground. Ben had grown over the past few months, and he was even taller than Mia than he had been. When Mia had fallen, he'd grabbed her and apparently succeeded in ensuring that she never hit the ground a little too well. "Sorry," he apologized, setting her down.

Still red, he grinned and bent at the waist in a small bow. "Shall we, My Lady?" he asked in a mocking tone, holding out his arm.

"Of course, we shall." Mia place her hand in the crook of his elbow, as Trin had taught them. As they approached the doors, she whispered, "You're mocking me, Ben."

Ben laughed gently. The front doors were already opened wide for them, with the doormen bowing lowly. Once they got inside, a servant bowed and guided them through the corridor. They didn't speak, for they didn't want him to hear anything they may have to say.

After several minutes of being led through twisting corridors, they came to what were obviously the doors to the ballroom. Bowing again, the servant left them, going back to see to other arrivals. Another pair of servants stood just inside the doors and opened them wide for the new guests.

The sight beyond was indescribably beautiful, and both Ben and Mia had a very good view from the top of a grand staircase. Every woman in the room was in an ornate ball gown. There were many different styles, and especially colors. There were so many different colors in each cluster of people that it was hard to know which person was wearing what. The men were wearing tuxedos remarkably similar to Ben's. Their shirts were mostly white, but the suits came in a variety of colors. Many were wearing one color layered over another.

A short, stout man bustled over to Ben and Mia impatiently. "Names?" he inquired. He was the announcer, the man that would proclaim their names across the hall for all to hear.

Ben glanced at Mia, not sure what she would do. She couldn't afford to let King Dimitri know of her arrival just yet.

"Natalie Kale," Mia answered without hesitation. She watched Ben for his response.

Thinking through a slight haze of panic, Ben looked at Mia. *Should I use a fake name?* he thought desperately. He glanced up at the impatient man and back at Mia, who saw his panic and shook her head slightly.

"Your name," she mouthed to him, making sure the announcer wouldn't notice.

Ben nodded slightly, reassured. "Benjamin Grenville," he informed the short man, who nodded.

Stepping back onto his small lectern, the herald took a

deep breath and shouted, "Lady Natalie Kale and her escort, Benjamin Grenville!" Only a few pairs of eye turned their way, and the herald sighed.

It must get so dull doing that, Mia thought. *No wonder why he's so snappy.* She linked her arm in Ben's and started down the stairs, Ben right beside her. No one was dancing, but many people were deep in conversation. "I wonder why nobody is dancing," Mia said at the bottom of the stairs, loud enough for the closest knot of people to hear them.

A young woman and her escort turned. She had blonde, curly hair that was tied back, and was wearing a black mask, gloves, and a dress of both deep green and black. Her escort had on a matching outfit. His auburn hair clashed a little with the coloring, but he looked all right and appeared perfectly happy to be attending with the beautiful girl on his arm.

"I believe that we have to wait for King Dimitri to arrive and formally announce the beginning of the ball," the woman said, smiling radiantly. "My name is Sasha Atwood of Amaria. Was that you just announced?"

Mia smiled warmly and nodded. "I am Natalie Kale; this is my escort, Ben Grenville. We came from the south edge of Mabec. Ben went into town one day and saw the poster up for the ball; otherwise we wouldn't have known about it at all," she explained, giggling.

Ben admired Mia's explanation. She had told the truth, but only the parts that were convenient to share.

Sasha's smile became more genuine, rather than politely interested. "Really? I wasn't aware that people came from *all* over Iceworld!" Her escort pulled on her gloved hand and gave her a pointed look. "Sorry! This is my escort, Jason Quip. Please forgive him for not introducing himself; he is mute and cannot."

Ben broke in with a laugh before Mia could speak again. "I apologize," he laughed, addressing Jason, when faced with two very outraged expressions from the ladies. "It is just that, even if you hadn't been mute, we probably wouldn't get a word in edgewise with these two." He started to grin, as did Jason.

Mia opened her mouth to say a well-formed retort when a blast of trumpets filled the air, demanding all of the guests' attention.

Chapter 21: The Dance

Everybody turned at the sound of the fanfare. At the top of the steps, the announcer took his position. Taking a deep breath, he boasted at the top of his lungs, "His Royal Majesty, King Dimitri of Iceworld!" At his announcement, the double doors swung open, and the king stepped forward. He stared down at his subjects, his face left uncovered.

A lifeless mumble went through the crowd, "Long live the king!"

King Dimitri was dressed lavishly in dull tones. His entire suit was dark hues of grays and blacks with a white shirt. He had on a black tuxedo jacket with a gray vest and pants. A silver crown studded with diamonds perched on his head. He looked imperially down at the crowd as if daring them to break the silence that had followed their well-wishing for him.

Mia slid surreptitiously behind Ben, avoiding being seen by the king as his gaze swept the room. Ben opened his mouth to quietly pick on her, to cheer her back up, when he felt a sharp elbow knock into his. Looking in the direction of the nudge, he saw Jason with a serious expression shaking his head gently, obviously telling Ben not to say anything.

Ben nodded to Jason, grateful for the tip, and turned back to King Dimitri. By now he had descended the stairs and arrived at his throne, which was sitting to one side of the ballroom.

Before sitting down, the king turned to the crowd. Throwing his arms open wide, he smiled warmly. It was a smile never reaching his eyes. "Honored guests, I thank you from the bottom of my soul for appearing before me tonight. Some of you have come farther than others; it is unfortunate, and I can only express my regret that it must have been an uncomfortable journey and my desire for you to make yourselves comfortable and to enjoy yourselves." King Dimitri bowed deeply and sat, his speech finished, and waved to the small orchestra to begin playing.

A reluctant cheer rose from the crowd; it was a moment before people managed to make their throats work enough to make an enthusiastic sound. Apparently, it wasn't King Dimitri they came to support, just his ball.

Suddenly, there was a flurry of hundreds of moving colors as people wishing to dance stepped forward with their partners. Sasha tugged on Jason's arm. Bowing to her, he held out his arm out to her, which she happily took, to escort her onto the dance floor; they soon disappeared in between the swirling colors.

Ben turned to Mia and bowed deeply. When he came back up, a smile lit his face completely. Mia smiled back at him, knowing that he was about to say something to make her laugh.

With his head tilted at a vain angle, Ben inquired in a mocking tone, "My Lady, would you honor me with a dance?" holding out his own hand to her.

Mia smirked and placed her hand in his. "Of course I will, Ben," she responded. When they reached the dance floor, she looked at him with a fake disdainful expression, and sniffed. "You are mocking me again."

Still beaming, Ben laughed and shrugged. "Oh, and what reason do I have for that?" he asked jokingly as they prepared to dance. All that was left was a swell in the music for Ben to sweep her into the dance.

"Since when do you *need* a reason, Ben?" Mia laughed as well.

Ben opened the dance by taking the first step. Once they were in beat, he whirled Mia around and then stopped her abruptly, close enough for her to hear him. "You're right, I don't need one, but I have to. It's my job to cheer you up when you're upset." The dance continued and Ben was forced to twirl Mia away again. When he caught her again, her expression was tense and agitated. "Stop thinking about later; it'll only bother you. You have talent; you *can* do this. For now, have fun. The hard part doesn't come until all the guests leave."

The dance caused them to separate and switch partners. Ben found himself dancing with a brown-haired girl in red while Mia was across from a flamboyantly dressed young man in a tux of deep orange. The suit itself seemed very out of place, and Ben could hear his strange accent from where he was dancing.

The accented man bent down and said something to Mia quietly. Her face twisted into a smile, and Ben felt his gut tighten. However, as he and his oblivious partner came

Iceworld

closer to Mia and the strange man, he could see that the man had made Mia laugh but hadn't relieved her anxiety. Mia was still tense as she was returned to Ben, but she relaxed a little around him.

The dance ended softly, with an overly-flourished twirl. As Ben executed this, he couldn't help but smile as he held Mia carefully, as needed. Whenever they had practiced this dance in the mountain, Mia had gotten lightheaded by the end.

Smiling back up at him, Mia started to continue their previous conversation. "That was awfully kind of you to say that," she said, inspecting him. "Now, would you mind telling me who you are and what you have done with my escort?" she questioned, her grin not quite serious enough to mean it.

Ben laughed. "Oh, I haven't done anything..." A grin grew on his face as he continued. "He's probably hanging around here somewhere," he added jokingly as they went to sit down.

Mia shook her head disbelievingly and stared out at the many hues flashing by. "Aren't they beautiful?" she asked quietly, her eyes sparkling as she stared, entranced by the dancers.

Ben, who had also been watching the dancers, glanced at her and then back again, his expression set grimly. "Yes, they are." He wanted to tell her that she surpassed them all, but hadn't yet opened his mouth to say it when Sasha and Jason spilled out of the throng of people, flushed and smiling.

Sasha immediately sat beside Mia and started talking animatedly to her about how everyone in Amaria had been forced to learn the dance so that they would be able to do it at the ball; they apparently didn't have it in the vivacious woman's hometown. Mia sympathized with her.

"My uncle had to show Ben and me how to hold our own in all of these dances. Apparently, the last King and Queen threw a lot of balls, and he went to most of them," she made up wildly. Thinking about it, it was probably entirely true. "We studied them for nearly two months." She and Sasha continued to chat about the ball.

Looking bemused, Jason sat on Sasha's other side. Shooting a look at Ben, Jason smirked over the girls' heads. Ben returned the look and chuckled.

Soon a new song started, and Jason whirled Sasha away through the crowd. "Her feet will be killing her by the end of the night," Mia pointed out, smiling. There was a hint of jealousy in her tone as she watched them twirl away.

Ben smiled and started to offer to take her onto the dance floor, but then a handsome, young man stepped toward them and bowed deeply to Mia. She looked shocked and glanced at Ben uncomfortably.

"May I have this dance, beautiful lady?" the young man asked charmingly. He had ebony hair, strong jaw line, and hazel eyes. His golden vest glimmered faintly under the sharp black jacket that fit so well that it showed his muscles in the best light possible.

Ben's defenses immediately bristled. He didn't like this man or how suave he was being toward Mia. Mia smiled tightly and took a deep breath, shooting Ben a glance as she stood, curtsying to the man. "It is truly up to my escort. Perhaps you should ask him," she replied unsteadily. Her hands shook, not sure whether this was a trick or just some arrogant young peacock who simply wanted to dance with her.

Ben nodded stiffly, standing and putting a comforting hand on Mia's elbow. "I suppose I cannot keep her to myself.

Go ahead," he answered eloquently. As the charismatic young man swept Mia away and into the dance, he threw Ben a condescending and triumphant expression. Ben decided immediately that he didn't like the man behind the mask.

Mia was twirled around forcefully by the man, sometimes becoming uncomfortably dizzy. He continuously talked about himself. She learned that his name was Brian Call. He was well-born, was very wealthy, and danced very well. Once, they twirled past a very surprised looking Sasha who was dancing with Jason.

Flashing a quick, inquisitive look at Brian for Mia to see, Sasha was forced to wait for an answer. The music was fast, and it took a lot of concentration to be able to keep up. At the end of the dance, Mia was worn out and flushed from the exertion. Brian grinned at her and was about to say something when Ben cut in, right on cue. "I believe it is my turn for her hand in a dance," he asserted, giving Brian a smug look as he shouldered his way between them, and faced Mia.

For a moment, Brian's charming demeanor was broken as Ben stepped between them, and he stood looking at Ben with disdain. Nevertheless, the young man bowed before he left, seeming slightly disgruntled but just as suave as before.

Ben took his place just as a slow, steady waltz picked up. The musicians seemed to be making up for the increased pace of the previous dance with the relaxed pace of this one. Looking around, as if disinterested, Ben inquired, "So did you enjoy the last dance?" trying to sound as aloof as he'd like to be.

Mia looked at him carefully for a moment before answering. "Why do you care to know?" she questioned, an eyebrow raised expectantly at him. She had liked the man even less than Ben had and couldn't understand what had her friend so riled up.

Throwing a look down at her, Ben executed a delicate and beautiful turn instead of answering; Mia laughed gently and tilting her head away from him, grabbing back onto him for balance. "He was very formally polite, Ben. Nice, but he said nothing too deep or funny. Brian's charming, but completely self-centered; he only talked about himself." Smiling, Mia turned her face toward Ben's. "I'd still like to know why you care," she added.

Suddenly confronted by her crystal blue eyes, Ben had to think quickly to come up with a suitable answer. "Because you're uncle would have my head if I didn't keep an eye on you. You have to be careful to avoid attention. We don't want the king to notice you too early, now do we?" he pointed out. "And you don't know who you can trust here. For all you know, he could be one of the king's men."

Mia rolled her eyes at him. "Oh, what a way to get my mind off the problem, Ben!" she muttered in a sarcastic undertone. She quickly became moody and avoided meeting Ben's eye again.

Realizing his error, "Come on, you know I have a point." The music suddenly swelled and slowed down, gently tapering to the end.

As they stopped dancing, Mia nodded incredulously. "I suppose. Let's sit down." Deep in thought, she walked over to their seats.

"Would you really rather I said something else?" Ben asked, making things up as he went along. He decided to do the most daring thing he'd imagined. "No, I'm sorry Mia. I wasn't being completely honest." He sat Mia down seriously, looking into her eyes with a solemn expression.

Mia stared at him, waiting for him to go on.

"I'm in love with you, Mia. Looking at you dancing with him made me the most jealous I've ever been in my life," he stated. His tone was calm and expressionless, and he made the corners of his mouth curve up playfully.

Mia stared at him and then down at the curving of his lips. Her own wide smile started forming and grew until she was laughing. Ben started laughing too, and Mia swatted him on the arm.

"Ben, you're horrible! You really had me going. If it weren't for your stupid grin, I would have believed you!" Ben laughed with her as she calmed down, but he was having problems relaxing.

After several minutes, Mia glanced up to look at the king. At first, she thought that there was no one on the throne. A second, more careful look told her that she was entirely correct. "Where's the king?" she asked Ben, her voice rising in panic. Scanning the room frantically, Mia felt as if her eyes were going to pop out of her head in concern.

Ben followed her gaze and saw the empty throne. "I dunno," he answered bluntly. Searching the crowd, he spotted the gray suit bobbing through the crowd. "Oh, there he is," Ben indicated the direction.

Mia looked to where he was pointing and shrank back a little, though she relaxed. "Is he coming this way?" she probed, trying to hide herself behind Ben. It seemed to her that every few beats of the music brought King Dimitri closer to their seats.

Ben shook his head. King Dimitri had joined the latest dance; his partner looked very discomfited yet flattered that he had chosen her. "The trick is going to be keeping an eye on him. I have a feeling that it will be easier for me than you," he added. The king wasn't the only man out looking for a beautiful girl to dance with. Ben saw another young man making his way through the crowd toward Mia.

Mia looked puzzled, not noticing the man making a beeline for her. "Why do you say that?" She had scarcely spoken when the young man stepped forward and asked for her hand in the next dance.

Ben laughed and consented, giving Mia a pointed look as she walked away. He was content to watch King Dimitri for a while. However, he was also careful to keep an eye on Mia and the various men she danced with by the end of the evening.

The king seemed to be switching partners several times per dance. There became a sort of pattern. The routine would start with King Dimitri walking towards a young woman. The announcer would whisper her name in his ear and leave. The king would bow and ask to cut in, to which the answer was always yes. No one was stupid enough to say no.

While Mia was dancing, Ben watched the king. When Ben and Mia danced together, they convinced Sasha and Jason to rest and keep an eye on where the king was.

On one such time, Mia and Ben returned to their seats to find Jason sitting alone, staring glumly at the floor. Ben looked at him curiously. "Where's Sasha?" he asked.

Unable to speak, Jason simply made a vague hand gesture toward the dance floor, indicating that she was dancing. Looking up, both Ben and Mia saw that Sasha was dancing with the king, and the poor girl was looking more and more uncomfortable by the second.

Putting a hand on Jason's shoulder, Mia tried to comfort him. "Oh, Jason, she'll be back soon. King Dimitri doesn't dance with anyone for very long," she explained.

As predicted, the king was soon escorting Sasha back

Iceworld

to her seat. "Thank you, Lady, for allowing me the pleasure of dancing with you," he said dully, but eloquently, bowing to her. He was obviously uninterested in such formalities.

After a mumbled response from Sasha, King Dimitri turned to Mia. The announcer was immediately at his elbow and whispered something in his ear before disappearing again. A lackluster smile appeared on the king's face as he attempted to be warm.

"Lady Natalie, would your escort mind if I were to steal you away for this dance?" he inquired with a lifted tone.

Ben bowed to the king as Mia curtsied. "Of course, Your Majesty. If you wish it," he responded formally. Sitting back down, Ben thought about what he really wanted to say to King Dimitri: "Actually, I do mind. I personally don't want her anywhere near a raving lunatic murderer like you," but he didn't dare say it out loud. It would only bring them heaps of trouble.

Mia raised herself out of her deep curtsy. "Good evening, Sire," she said meekly in a very unfamiliar voice. As the king offered a hand, she flinched almost imperceptibly, but forced herself to allow him to take her to the dance floor.

Not noticing the small flinch, the swift, oily man pulled Mia along as if he'd done this too many times to care much about which woman he was pulling behind him.

After they began to dance, King Dimitri never once looked at Mia. "Do you like the ball so far, Lady Natalie?" he asked nonchalantly.

Mia stared over his shoulder. "Yes, Sire. It is the only one I have ever been to. It was... kind of you to host such a marvelous event in your own home," she replied, barely managing to choke out the word 'kind.'

King Dimitri, still unobserving and uncaring, kept his

eyes riveted to the passing walls as they danced. "Why, thank you for the compliment. It is very kind of you to say that." After he spoke, there was a long silence that Mia didn't dare break, but she felt as if she had to keep him from actually finding a bride. She had to say something to catch his interest.

"On the way here, Sire, my escort and I saw 'Wanted' posters. Might I ask who you are searching for?" she questioned as they danced on. The song seemed to be taking forever.

The king still didn't face her as he responded. "Ah, it is merely a trifling matter. Nothing to worry about. The fugitives will be captured and brought to justice soon enough."

Mia frowned. "I hardly think justice is the word for it," she blurted out before she could stop herself. She realized what she had said, but it was too late to take it back. Determinedly, she stared off into the distance, not meeting the eyes of her mother's murderer.

Momentarily, King Dimitri's eyebrows creased into a frown, but they returned to normal shortly. When he answered, his voice was raised slightly, as if he were asking a very delicate question. "And what *would* you call it, Lady Natalie?" he asked. He was interested now, yet deceptively aloof.

Thinking hard, Mia came up with what she wanted to say to him in words appropriate enough for the delicate situation she was in. Suddenly, she was very aware of the guards posted on the sides of the ballroom and how cold and clammy the king's hand was upon her waist. "I would say that you rule your country with fear by your side. Your subjects fear you and the power you hold, rather than obeying you out of sheer respect," she replied carefully. "I don't think that you have done anything to deserve these people's respect."

Eyes narrowed, the king turned to face her at last, scrutinizing her. "That is a very bold statement for one so young. Who has taught you these things?" he interrogated her. His expressionless mask returned, hiding his physical emotions, but suspicion laced his words heavily.

"Oh, I form my own opinions through observation. That particular one was developed quite recently." Feeling she had said too much, Mia stopped talking; the king was suddenly far too interested in her.

Shortly after, the song finally ended. Abandoning her former plan, Mia made to curtsy to the king and return to Ben quickly and let the king dance with whomever he liked, but King Dimitri caught her elbow. "Please, accompany me outside," he told her, pulling her along. Mia, realizing that it wasn't a simple request, barely had time to glance over her shoulder as the crowd parted before them.

As they stepped up to the railing on the terrace, Mia was hit with a blast of cold air. She looked out over Snowsdale, aware that the king was watching her closely, analyzing every move she made. Intensely aware of the things going on around her, Mia heard him move to lean on the railing as he inspected her. "You've grown in the past months, Princess," he stated.

Chapter 22: Discovery

Mia froze as the king used her title. She could feel his gaze penetrating her mask and burning her cheek from where he was standing to her left. Gathering her courage, she snorted derisively and quipped, "Really? You seem the same as when I left. A greedy, cruel, jealous man that calls himself a king."

King Dimitri's countenance grew dangerously dark as he scowled at her. "I would enjoy nothing more than to make you suffer for that little dig right here and now; if only it weren't for the fact that all my guests would witness it," he snarled. His eyes glinted steely, making him look even icier than before.

Mia rolled her eyes, as if she weren't frozen with fear. "I'll remember that the next time you try to kill me. And just how did you plan to find a wife and have a child before

I got my hands on you?" she questioned, doing her best to make ice drip from the threat. "There'd be no woman who would have you; even one who was blind *and* deaf."

"Why you... Do you really think you could best me?" asked the king, lowering his voice with each word. It had become a low snarl that seemed to spout from some deep fountain of hatred. "I only half expected to lure you out with this ruse. The other half of me said that you weren't this stupid. I suppose I was wrong." He frowned at Mia deeply. "You know, I never really thought that Trin was dead. I suspect he informed you about the more intricate details of being royalty. Of course, he would have immediately told you that you had to move by tonight, for fear of losing the crown." He paused for the impact of this to sink in. "It was a very neatly set trap, don't you think, *Princess*?" he asked, putting venom laced emphasis on 'Princess.'

Mia shrugged as if she had known it was a trap the entire time. Mentally, she was reeling. He'd only been luring her here. He wasn't looking for a bride at all; the king only wanted to ensure that she was going to return to the castle. "I suppose. Off to the dungeon again, I suspect?" she questioned mockingly. "Give an apology to Quimble for me for locking him down there."

The king glared at her heavily, hating her smug expression. Then Mia found herself staring at the blank wall of the dungeon once again.

*   *   *   *

Ben paced and glanced anxiously around the ballroom. King Dimitri had moved on to a new partner with an agitated expression, but Mia hadn't come back. There was no sign of her anywhere, and Ben couldn't help but feel apprehensive. Neither Sasha nor Jason had seen her either, though they both solemnly agreed to stay on the lookout for her.

Hours passed and the crowd thinned, but the three stayed a little longer, asking if anyone had seen a beautiful girl that looked like Mia. Finally, Sasha apologized and left with Jason, who shrugged apologetically as he followed her out. Ben thanked them and turned back to scanning the ballroom for his friend.

While he didn't see Mia, there was a rather distraught looking woman wringing her hands and searching the ballroom just as ardently as he. He stepped up behind the lost looking maiden. "Who are you looking for?" he asked gently, putting on a kind smile.

The woman, flustered and confused, turned toward him. "Oh! My escort seems to have disappeared on me. His name is Brian. He was wearing a black and gold suit, and he... Oh, there he is!" she cried, waving her arms at the charming gentleman who had danced with Mia earlier.

Brian gave Ben a short nod of recognition and linked his arm in the lady's nonchalantly. He didn't seem to have much interest in her, and Ben guessed that he had only asked her to the ball so that he wouldn't have to come alone. "Well, hello again. How fares your companion?" he asked politely, a less than polite grin slowly forming on his face.

Ben tried hard to fight the urge to punch the smug character. Frowning, he responded curtly, "She seems to have disappeared."

Brian nodded slowly. "How unfortunate. Well, I hope that you have better luck keeping her under control next time, then." With that he nodded and left, pulling the lady by her arm out of the ballroom.

Ben grimaced and watched him leave. As he turned, a hunched-over servant scuttled up to him, bowing low. "Do you need anything, sir?" he asked politely.

Ben cast another searching look around the room before answering. "Yes, have you perhaps seen a black-haired young lady in a blue dress? I cannot seem to find her anywhere," he explained.

The king was walking past when Ben was speaking to the servant. Upon hearing Mia's description, stopped and looked very carefully at Ben. Ben and the servant both bowed low as the king, in a very aloof voice, inquired, "Lady Natalie Kale?" Ben straightened and nodded. "Actually, she wasn't feeling at all well when our dance ended. I offered her a room here in the palace and she accepted. She will be sent home by the Counsel of Magic just as soon as she has made a full recovery."

The servant backed a few steps away as it became apparent that it was going to be a private conversation between the king and Ben. "That is very gracious, Your Majesty, but duty binds me to wait for her until she is well enough to travel," Ben replied. All sorts of terrible things that could have befallen Mia flashed across his mind. "If you don't mind, Sire, I would like to stay here and then return home with her at my side."

Nodding, King Dimitri showed no expression other than polite annoyance. Then a small, fleeting smile passed his face. "Of course you may stay here. You can see her tomorrow." He gestured for the servant standing behind Ben to come forward. "Prepare a room for this young man. He is a guest and will be treated as such until the lady is ready to see him." The servant nodded and scuttled away.

Turning back to Ben, the king inspected him, walking in a circle around him. Ben couldn't help but feel that the cold, penetrating eyes were like those of a vulture, just waiting to tear him to pieces. "Forgive me for prying, but have you known Natalie Kale very long?" he questioned.

Ben thought carefully. "To be entirely honest, Sire, we met a while ago, months even, but I feel as if I never know much about her. She is a mystery to me."

King Dimitri nodded, a small smile playing around the corners of his lips. "So you are in love with this girl, then?"

Ben shrugged, suddenly even more wary of this viper. Just then, the servant returned, saying that the room was prepared and that he could show Ben to his room. King Dimitri smiled. "All right then, I'll let you get some rest. Perhaps in the morning you will be able to see your lady fair." His grin was somewhat malicious, and he whispered into the servant's ear before he left.

The servant nodded and motioned for Ben to come with him. Following him out of the ballroom and up and down passages, Ben realized how easy it would be to get lost in the palace. They reached his bed chamber, the one with a door slightly ajar.

Stepping in, Ben walked over to sit on the bed. It was soft and downy, nothing like anything he'd ever been on before. The servant bowed nervously as he closed the door behind him. Ben, from the bed, heard something click in the door. He'd been locked in. Jumping up, he pounded on the door to no avail. No one was going to help him.

Chapter 23:
Unhappy Incentive

To Mia, the long wait in the dungeon was daunting, and it stretched on endlessly without anything to do. She paced, waited, hummed, and sang, drowning her own fear and apprehension. Her main concern was what the king was planning for her and what had happened to Ben. Had he left? Or hidden himself somewhere in the palace? Was he captured?

Knowing Ben wouldn't leave her to her fate did nothing to improve her already guilty conscience. Not daring to try magic, Mia was helpless and could do nothing until she was let out of the dungeon. Lying down, she fell into a fitful sleep.

Mia walked up and down the unlit corridors, each wall lined with doors. She'd tried to open them, but they were all locked. As she turned a corner, she saw a single door at the end of the corridor. Trying the handle, Mia found it unlocked and pushed open the door so that she could escape the black tunnel. Light burst forth, blossoming to engulf her and momentarily blinding her.

As it faded, Mia opened her eyes cautiously. She saw a tall, beautifully radiant woman with dark hair sitting beside her. Their feet were dangling in the cool water while they sat in the shade of a sweeping tree that leaned toward the water; its leaves dipping below the surface. Nearby was the park's boardwalk and the soft, grassy ground broke off into the lake that rippled gently in the breeze.

Mia was a six year old little girl, happy and smiling for no other reason than to smile. The woman holding her hand was more than beautiful. She had long black hair tied away from the crystal blue eyes that were set into her soft, creamy-skinned face.

"Isn't this nice, Princess?" the woman asked, smiling as she spoke. "The sun is shining, and the day is warm and breezy. It's a perfect day for a picnic." Her voice was soft and distant, the memory making it distant. Mia flashed her own smile up at the relaxed woman in the cut-off shorts beside her.

"Yes, Mommy. Can we go swimming yet?" she whined, wiggling her toes in the placid water, starting a small wake.

Diane Snow's smile brightened, wiggling her toes as well. "Shouldn't we wait for Daddy? He's bringing all the fun toys! Or don't you want them?" She laughed, the sound filling the air like a flute. She reached out to hug her little daughter.

Mia sighed and slumped away from the hug, sticking her hands in the water. She had her swimsuit on, but her father, Simon Snow, hadn't arrived yet.

Diane saw the look on Mia's face and sighed, wanting to cheer the little girl up. "Or, instead, we could just... tickle!" she laughed, wiggling her fingers into Mia's stomach.

Mia shrieked and squirmed left and right, only getting tickled even more. She finally managed to break free of her mother's grasp, only to fall straight into the shallow water.

As she hit the surface, the memory changed. Instead of sitting in the water at the beach with her mother, Mia found herself sitting in her bedroom, tears spilling down her cheeks in fear and pain. In this memory, she was eight years old, her mother having died little less than a year ago.

She held two things in her hands, one of them was her mother's favorite small snowflake necklace, and the other was a picture of her mother that had been taken a few years ago. It was when Diane had decided to bake a cake, at which she had hopelessly failed, having fun the entire time. In the picture she had flour on her face, and her hair was pushed up into a spiky knob on the back of her head. She was laughing and smiling, something she wouldn't do again, ever. It was a slightly tattered old photo, but it was the only thing she had left of her mother beside the necklace.

Mia could hear her father downstairs, raging as he threw dresses, jewelry, and anything else of his wife's into a pile to be either sold or burnt. Sobs tore straight from her chest as she lay on her floor, trying to deny what was happening. Her father had had these fits before. It had started the day her mother died. The death was having an effect on her too, but what was happening to her father was scary.

Suddenly, her head hurt as she was yanked into the air. The picture and necklace fell to the floor, far away from her. Screaming, she tried to pull away, but her hair was locked into a firm, tugging grip.

Mia woke up with a scream as the guard tugged yet again on her hair. Her mask slid over her wet face; she'd been crying in her sleep. She was dragged out of the cell by the rough guard, who then shoved her to her feet and pushed her along the corridor. "Go on, keep moving," he ordered her gruffly. Mia moved stiffly up the stairs, rubbing her scalp.

The passages seemed vaguely familiar to Mia as she was marched along. She realized that the guard was taking her to the study, the place she had been on her first 'visit' to the castle when she had first met the king.

When they reached the study, Mia saw that the guard had been changed back. He was no longer green and had been returned to his normal form. Mia wasn't laughing when she went in this time. Instead, she was terribly angry; her vengeance flaring up violently. Her dream had reminded her of how strong her hatred for the king was.

The guard marched her to the back of the study, where there was a large area that was completely roped off from the more scholarly part of the room. It seemed to be a practice area, clear of any shelves, books, or scrolls. It stretched across the entire back wall and had several windows letting in early morning light. This roped off area was where King Dimitri stood waiting.

Fuming, he paced back and forth. When Mia was shoved into his audience, still wearing her ball gown, he turned to face her directly, his face screwed up in rage. He raised a hand and slapped her across the face with as much force as he could muster. "That was for your impudence last night," he whispered in her ear, his voice sounding as if it would cut into her.

Pulling away, he looked at her with such loathing that she stepped back, nervous. "Give up your claim to the throne," he commanded venomously.

Mia laughed as coldly as she could, her face smarting as she did. Feeling the guard shift uncomfortably at her high pitched cackle, Mia was heartened knowing that she could get under his skin. "What makes you think that I would do that, you lazy pig? I've seen and met people from all over this world, and you haven't helped a single person in that whole lot. Why should a cruel tyrant hold power over those whom he repels? Subjects used to come in and ask for guidance and advice. Now all of them are shut out, unless you gain something from it. You're not only a coward for striking a helpless woman but also a worthless worm."

King Dimitri's eyes grew wide with rage and he raised his hand to strike her again. This time, as his hand struck, Mia was knocked sideways across the floor, landing in an undignified heap. "I wouldn't be so confident if I were you," the king drawled smugly, striding around slowly so that she would have to turn to watch him. "Your life is in my hands; I could kill you at any second. Then no one would be in my way, little Princess."

Mia chuckled slightly. "I have friends, you know. Most of them would prefer to have me alive, and they could easily lead a rebellion," she said, looking up at him slowly, wiping a small trickle of blood from the corner of her mouth.

A cruel smile started to lift the edges of the king's mouth. "Speaking of your friends, I have a bit of an unhappy incentive for you."

The doors swung open and two guards came in, frog-marching a struggling young man between them. They stopped and turned him around roughly, exposing the man's face. "Let me go! You can't handle me like this! I have rights!"

"Ben!" Mia cried.

Ben's eyes snapped up to meet hers, and his righteous anger turned into alarmed relief. "Mia!"

Mia stood and started to run towards him but was seized by another dutiful guard who stood with an expressionless face, and his hands clamped on her upper arms. Trying to wrench her arm free, Mia growled under her breath. "Let him go!" she demanded, facing the king. "He has *nothing* to do with this!"

It was King Dimitri's turn to laugh. "You aren't in a position to order me to do anything. Beside, you'll find that he has *everything* to do with this," he said, menace oozing out of every glance and movement. "You have a serious choice that some must make, Princess. Now either pick your friend here," he indicated Ben by placing a hand on his shoulder, which was still being pulled by the guards, making Ben jerk away from him in disgust, "or the throne. It's really your choice, but you *will* die, one way or another."

Mia, formulating a plan, answered slowly. "You want to know why you're so horrible? You take joy in pain. It's probably why you killed my mother. Or perhaps it was greed or jealousy?"

The smile slid from the king's face quicker than oil. "Your *mother* was a fool. She picked an inbred, common *whelp* for a husband. Then she ran from power and had her horrible little daughter that no one cared about enough to look for."

Mia would have shouted at him, but she controlled her anger and let him continue. He was now in the middle of a monologue, and she had to keep him distracted if she wanted to save both Ben and herself. Besides, if she said anything too upsetting to King Dimitri, he might kill Ben

Iceworld

just to spite her. She was slowly working her magic, using it to help Ben as the king spoke.

"She wasn't meant to rule!" the king ranted on, stepping away from Ben. "I was! Diane ran from her world, and I was the one who stayed. I am the ruler of Iceworld, and no little girl will defeat me!" His voice was growing louder and louder as he went on, rising to a shout.

Mia refused to back down or even flinch as the king started storming toward her. She dared a glance at Ben who was still held by the guards, but he didn't seem so strained. The guards hadn't moved since the king had stepped away from them, and their expressions were blank and still; they weren't even blinking. It was amazing to watch.

Dimitri continued to yell directly in Mia's face, forcing her to look back at him. "Do you really think you can best me? I have the crown and the power. You'd never heard of Iceworld until you got trapped here! There is no possible way that you could have learned nearly enough magic to even pretend that you can match me!"

The guard's hands holding Mia were still, unmoving, and stone-like. Delicately, so as to not disrupt the petrifying spell she had placed on him, she pulled her arms free. The spell would last as long as he wasn't moved.

"Yes, I do actually. If I didn't believe I could beat you, there would be no possible way that I could." She pulled herself up to her full height, making herself just as big as she wanted to feel. "I'll face you now, here," she pronounced as Ben too pulled himself free.

Expression wild, King Dimitri glanced furiously at the guards, who still hadn't moved. He regained his composure and smirked at her. "Very smooth, petrified?" he asked, forcing his voice not to betray any alarm. He ran his hand through his blonde hair and grimaced at her. "You have talent, no mistaking that, but still no chance against me." Suddenly, he turned, raising his arms. As Mia watched, he shot a blast of icy shards toward Ben, who evaded the worst of the danger. However, he couldn't dodge all of it. One particularly jagged shard struck him in the calf. Blood flowed dark against his black suit, visible only because of the red stained skin exposed.

Ben stumbled, gasping and his hand clutched around the shard. Braving the pain and yanking it out, he groaned and fell to his knees. Rage swelled inside Mia, and she raised a shield to keep him from the fight. Aiming a powerful curse directly at the king, she missed as he made his own shield to block it. "I'm the one you have to worry about! Not him!" she yelled at the king, her adrenaline pumping through her veins faster than was probably safe.

The king looked at her calmly and nodded solemnly. "You are right, *Princess*. I *should* be dealing with you!" Raising his arms, he did the same to her, planning to kill.

Chapter 24: Sorcerer's Duel

Mia managed to protect herself just before the spell hit her. She felt the bone jarring thud of the curse breaking upon the shield. Crouched behind it, Mia gathered her strength as she felt King Dimitri hurl curse after curse at her.

Concentrating, Mia briefly ducked from behind her make-shift cover and ricocheted one of his spells, unsteadying him. The king attacked even stronger after he recovered, throwing waves upon waves of overlapping spells. Then the spells stopped coming.

Hiding again, Mia dared a look over her shoulder; the king stood on the far side of the room, simply staring at her. She cast a suspicious glance around as something flickered in the corner of her vision.

Next to the shelves, something had moved. Dropping her shield, Mia stood and concentrated on it. Books suddenly flew from their perches and hovered in midair. Thuds and shouted curses rang out as the books drove a second King Dimitri from his hiding place. Books circled around him while he flapped at them uselessly.

Mia felt her energy starting to drain. Letting any and every spell she had done fall, she watched as the books fell in a heap to the floor. The king stood smiling evilly at her as she watched him carefully. The second king started clapping sarcastically. Mia was overwhelmed by the power it must have taken for the king to create a doppelganger and started solving the question of which one was the real threat.

From behind her, the king's smarmy voice called out. "Well done, noticing my trick like that," he told her. Neither one of the two kings Mia was watching had spoken.

Turning cautiously to look behind her, Mia saw a third king step out from the bookshelves. "How are you doing that?" Mia asked with forced steadiness.

The second king stepped forward. "With more power than you possess," he responded mockingly.

"It confuses enemies easily. Very helpful," chimed the first.

Mia shook her head, trying clear it, "And if the enemy isn't confused?"

The third king stepped closer. "Well, that doesn't matter. Now, does it, Mia? Both you and I know that you are just as confused as I want you to be. It's hidden beneath your eyes. You haven't got a clue as to which one of us is the real one. It may be me..."

"Or me..." repeated the second, stepping forward.

"Perhaps it's me," the first chanted, striding forward

Iceworld

quickly taking his place in the circle.

Spinning in a tight circle, Mia realized that she was boxed in. The required amount of power to sustain the spell must be draining King Dimitri, but what use was it to her if he managed to kill her? Turning around wildly, a half formulated plan started working in her mind. She turned so that she was facing one of the kings head on and had her back directly to another. She would probably regret the move, but she had to figure out which king was concrete.

Throwing herself backward, Mia rammed into a king as she shot a spell straight at the one in front of her. Both fell to the ground and instantly vanished. They were the magical illusions, and Mia now only had one king to deal with.

King Dimitri glared at her, enraged that she had figured out his spell and that he'd wasted so much energy for nothing. Furious, he shoved Mia away from him, ruining any chance she had to concentrate. Raising his arms for the final blow, the king started advancing on Mia with a look of supreme and malignant concentration upon his face.

Stumbling backward, Mia felt as if she were about to drop from exhaustion. She had very little magic left. Her vision was blurred with hot tears of defeat, denial and hatred. Completely undefended and exhausted, Mia tripped over the hem of the ball gown she was still wearing. As the edge dress ripped, Mia fell, landing hard on the hard, icy floor, crumbling into a pile.

The king continued to pursue her, menacingly fast. Inching away from him, Mia ran into the wall and found, with no small degree of panic, that she could go no farther. He had backed her into a corner.

Knowing he'd won, smelling his victory, the king grinned and started muttering spells under his breath. She could feel their malevolence in the air. Tensing, she realized that she was giving up. Her friends were counting on her; Ben's life counted on her, her father's sanity, too. There was no end to the things that needed her to win this fight.

Thinking of her friends, Mia's courage returned just as King Dimitri was about to release the magnified curse, the finishing strike. Squaring her shoulders and pushing herself to her feet, Mia drew from every energy reserve she had that was now fighting to be released. She could feel her life force flooding into her spell just before she thrust it out through her hands directly at the king. The power came gushing from her body as she let the barriers shatter in her mind. When the energy had all surged out of her, she slumped to the floor, completely drained.

The king screamed in agony as her curse struck him in the abdomen. His bloodcurdling wail went on and on as if he was on fire, dying, and refusing to let go of life.

Mia grimaced and clapped her hands over her ears, unsuccessfully trying to block out the terrible sound. It was the most raw, unharnessed power and pain she'd ever heard. She could feel her very soul retreating from the blight she'd caused on this man, though he deserved it. Feeling nauseous, Mia looked away from the king, for the sight of him was nothing pleasant.

King Dimitri's eyes were wide; he had an arm clamped around his stomach and was crouching, barely standing on his feet. He rocked back and forth between standing upright and being completely hunched over. The exposed skin on his hands and face was bubbling, boiling on his body, unable to contain him any longer. It had to end, and something whispered in her mind that it would only worsen unless she stopped it. However, Mia had no more control over her curse. It was doing its damage, and she was drained of everything she had left. She would die if the pain didn't kill the king first.

Trying to block out the scene, Mia tried to screw up her face and shut her eyes, but her tired muscles wouldn't respond. She was resigned to listen to the wailing and gruesome end of the king when she heard a large *THUD.* Then the horrible noise stopped. Mia opened her eyes cautiously.

Ben was standing where the king had been, with a large tome held in both hands, the blood on his pants still leaving a dark stain. A thin trail of blood led the way from where he had been to the shelf and then to the king, and it was now pooling around his ankle, gleaming and menacingly dark. He leaned heavily on his uninjured leg, looking down at the king's now lifeless form. Slowly, he raised his eyes to meet Mia's, incredulity and relief clearly written on his face.

Mia shook her head gently and lowered her eyes to look at King Dimitri. The body was faded from view and soon had vanished all together. Nothing remained of King Dimitri except the discontent, bitter feelings, and wounds he'd left behind.

Confused and tired, Mia laid down on the uncomfortable floor and closed her eyes. She felt Ben drop to his knees beside her, pulling her onto his lap as he sat stiffly on the ground. Sluggishly opening her eyes, Mia frowned at his leg, which was bleeding on the torn edge of her gown, staining the sky blue fabric red. "Let me heal that for you," she offered, starting to lift her hand over it and mutter the spell.

Ben pulled her back, snatching her hand away. "Oh, no you don't. You just won the duel. You were amazing, Mia, but you need sleep. Don't kill yourself healing a cut." When she was still about to protest, he put a hand to her mouth, covering it. "Rest, Mia. I'll be fine," he told her sternly. The leg would have normally made him grouchy and moaning, but he knew Mia had already come too close to killing herself that day.

Her black hair, which had fallen from the style she'd given it, now hung flat and covered part of her masked face. Behind the mask, her eyes were bleary and glassy and had the air of someone fighting off the sleepy subconscious.

"Mia, just go to sleep. You'll feel better once you do," Ben coaxed her, helping her take off her mask and brushing her hair behind her ear. He placed her head on his shoulder so that she wouldn't have to sleep against the hard wall.

Mia nodded sleepily against him. "That sounds good. I'll rest, heal your leg, and then we'll find Trin, Wizard and Katie," she told him and fell asleep.

Ben kept her close, taking in every moment he could. He wasn't going to let anything happen to her. "You were wonderful, Mia. You'll make a terrific Queen someday," he whispered, kissing her long hair. Mia was fast asleep and didn't hear him, but he thought he saw her smile in her dreams.

Chapter 25:
No Good-byes

Ben woke at the sound of footsteps coming across the floor, unaware that he had fallen asleep. Prickling in defense of this new threat, he saw a group of blue and white robed figures, both men and women, marching their way through the shelves. Glaring, Ben waited to see what they wanted.

One man stepped forward out of the knot of people, carefully avoiding the drying pool of blood on the floor, and addressed Ben in a loud voice. "Which one of you was the one that dethroned the king?" he questioned self-importantly.

Annoyed, Ben put a finger to his lips, indicating that he needed to be quiet and glanced at Mia, who continued to sleep. "Be quiet. She, Mia, did, and she needs rest." He frowned at the domineering man. "Just who are you anyway?"

The man bristled and held himself up to his full height. "I am Jed Silve, Head of the Royal Counsel of Magic," he responded brusquely, offended that this young man had never heard of him or known who he was.

"Well then, Jed," Ben acknowledged sarcastically, "Can we get Mia to a more comfortable room? Like I said, she needs rest."

Silve stared at Mia, debating with himself. It was obvious that he was hungry for answers, but knew he wouldn't get them if he tried to force them. Then his eyes grew wide. When he realized that Ben was still waiting for an answer, he asked in a gentle tone, "Is that a snowflake necklace around her neck?"

Barely glancing at Mia, Ben nodded. "Yes, she's the Ice Princess; King Dimitri himself wanted her out of the way so that he could rule unchallenged," he explained.

Silve's eyes widened as he kneeled; his companions doing the same. "The Princess's bedchambers will be prepared at once," he murmured in awe and reverence.

Ben stood up awkwardly, pulling Mia up with him and holding her upright, unsure about the sudden and dramatic change in the recently pompous man. Mia's eyes flickered briefly and a soft moan emanated from her. She put a hand to her head, which was pounding. "Are we captured again, Ben?" she asked, scared of the answer. Surely they were dead if not captured. But, then, why would her head hurt her so much if she was dead?

"No, not exactly, Mia. Open your eyes and see," he murmured in her ear with an emotion charged whisper.

Opening her eyes wider, Mia then noticed with slight alarm that a group of livery-clad people were kneeling at her feet. "Who're you?" she asked, sleepily ignorant, wondering who in Iceworld would want to bow to her.

"Your humble Counsel of Magic," Silve replied, "Your Highness."

"Oh." Mia's voice was soft and full of awe. It had just truly struck her what it meant that she had defeated the king.

"Your bedchamber is being prepared as we speak, Your Highness. You may go and rest there," Silve continued in his respectful tone as a maid walked in to lead Mia to her new room.

Mia hesitated and looked at Ben. Sluggishly, she started to ask, "Are you…"

Ben interrupted her, urging her forward with a little push. "Go, I'll be fine," he told her grudgingly. "I still have to go and get the others anyway."

Mia nodded and walked off with the maid, who was helping her walk upright.

Silve quickly healed Ben's leg for him and led him outside so he could summon Nomis. "You're all welcome to stay here in the palace," the counselor told him, inviting him with a kind smile and a clap on the arm. "You brought our dear princess back to us. It will be a while before people will believe it, but they will eventually."

*   *   *   *

Mia ran to Trin the next day as soon as she found him outside. Wizard, Katie, Trin and Ben had been waiting in the courtyard for her to wake up. Hugging her uncle, she grinned. "We won! We beat him, Trin!"

Trin laughed and returned the hug. "So I see! Well done. I'm so glad you're both all right." He smiled down at her and pushed his niece to her magic teacher so that Wizard could embrace her.

Katie jumped from Wizard's shoulder onto Mia's. "You

were gone a long time! Wizard and Trin were worried, but I knew you would be fine." She gave Mia the biggest hug she could muster around her neck. "I was wondering why you were taking so long about it, though!" she chatted away in Mia's ear. Undoubtedly, she'd found the wait dull.

Mia laughed. "You know, Katie, I actually missed the sound of your voice. I guess you're making up for lost time, huh?" She laughed again as Katie stuck out her little tongue at Mia.

Wizard stepped forward and embraced her new sovereign. "Great job, Mia. It's about time that he was struck down!" Releasing Mia with a curious expression, she inquired, "What happened to his um… body…anyway?"

Mia shrugged. "I'm not really sure. He got hit with one of my spells and was doubled over. Something horrible was going to happen, but then Ben clubbed him on the head with an enormous book. He collapsed from the combination, I guess. Then his body vanished before I even fell asleep. I have no clue why, but I'm glad he's gone." Mia smiled radiantly at Wizard, who seemed to have her doubts but smiled in return, forgetting them for the moment.

Ben, standing to the side, kept his bad news to himself for the moment. He'd been thinking more and more about something that was nagging at his mind, and he needed to decide what to do about it.

Mia noticed his glum expression, went over to him, and enveloped him in a hug also. "I couldn't have done it without you, Ben. Thanks," she whispered in his ear and giving him a brief peck on the cheek.

Ben turned flaming red and returned the hug, trying to ignore the foolish grins on the others' faces and the burning sensation from Mia's kiss. Pulling away, Ben gave her a tight smile, not wanting to ruin this day for her. When she didn't get a response, Mia bounced away, happy to relive her tale for her uncle and mentor.

Mia was the happiest that anybody had seen her. She hadn't had fresh air for three days, and it felt good to have the sun beat on her face and reflect off the snow around them. It seemed as if diamonds had been scattered across the ground by the way it sparkled. To add to the shimmering effect, Nomis lay not too far away, sunning himself.

Leaning against the dragon, Ben watched the others' reunion as they talked. Katie, Wizard, and Trin hadn't changed since the two had left for the mountain, but both Ben and Mia were given a change of clothes. Mia was in a beautiful lavender and pearl dress that was much more elegantly simple than her now tattered ball gown. A tiara sat on top of her shining black hair. Ben had dressed as he normally would, pants and a jacket to ward of the brisk chill of the palace courtyard.

Mia was talking animatedly to the others about the duel. Turning to flash a smile at him when she mentioned what he'd done, Mia kept telling her story. Katie and Wizard both wanted to hear about the ball and the dancing and the beautiful outfits.

Yet, there was something different about Mia now, different than any time Ben had known her. It wasn't long before he realized it was because she wasn't worried about anything for the first time. The entirety of their relationship, Mia had been worried about getting home, about getting out of prison, and then about the imminent duel between her and King Dimitri. Now that all of that stress was lifted from her shoulders, she seemed to glow with a previously subdued vivacity.

Knowing he was being selfish, and hating himself for

bringing Mia down on the one day she wouldn't have to worry, Ben pushed away from Nomis and strode hesitantly toward the small group.

"Hi, Ben! What's wrong?" Mia turned to him; her expression was one of confusion and concern, concern for him, wanting him to be happy, too.

Ben stood speechlessly looking at her for a moment, wanting this moment to last, so that she didn't have to be upset, but when she continued to wait, he sighed. He opened his mouth to say what needed to be said, but at first it wouldn't come out. Clearing his throat, he made himself say the words he knew she didn't want to hear. "Mia, I think I should go home. It's been almost six months since I left, and Mom's probably thinking the worst has happened to me."

Mia looked stunned, but then she brightened. "Of course, Ben! You can bring her back here, right?" she questioned, fearing the answer she knew she was getting.

Ben shook his head. "I'm afraid not. She doesn't even know about Nomis yet, and I can't just introduce her and expect her to get on. Besides, it's our home down there... We can't just leave it and never return."

Mia nodded. "That's fine, Ben. I completely understand. After all, this did just start out with you showing me the way here. Now you've gotten me here." She smiled sadly. "It just took a little longer than we expected." There was an edge in her voice indicating how sad she was.

Suddenly, a small, plotting smile grew in place of the sad one. Mia continued, "You know, I might be able to save you some time. Let me talk to the Counsel; maybe they'll help."

Ben nodded, wanting to hug her, but she ran away before he could say another word.

Iceworld

* * * *

Ben stroked one of the scales on Nomis's side with his thumb. The Counsel of Magic had grouped together with Wizard, as their leader, and Mia. They were standing in a straight line, hands linked, eyes closed, silently concentrating on something that no one else could see. They were trying to create a portal for Ben to get home quickly by passing through it. So far nobody could tell if it was working.

It started very small but grew quickly. A small silver spot high in the air started to spin, then red, blue, yellow, and violet streaks, fanned out from its center, making the light grow wider and higher. The colors all started spinning quickly and soon it became a large, silvery-white disk high above them.

When they finished, Mia walked over to Ben sadly. When Ben opened his mouth to speak, she held up her hand. "No good-byes, all right? They're too sad. You *will* come back eventually, even if I have to come down there myself and drag you through that portal," she informed him brusquely.

Ben grinned, shrugging. "That's fine by me. I don't like good-byes anyway. Though it might be better if you concentrated on everything you'll be doing here instead of what I'm doing," he pointed out.

Mia nodded fervently. "Probably, but you're my friend. I'll always have time, even if it's spent dragging you from one end of Iceworld to the other," she joked.

Laughing, Ben nodded. Hands in his pockets, he started to rock back and forth on his feet nervously. "I suppose I should get going. My mom is at the other end, and I'm starting to wonder what she's been doing all this time."

Mia sighed and looked at the portal with a grim

expression. "I guess so." Looking at Ben sadly, she added gently, "I'll miss you. Come back soon." She wrapped her arms tightly around his waist and gave him a final hug.

Wizard and Trin had also come to see Ben off and exchanged a small smile as they caught sight of their hug. Ben ignored them and hugged Mia back tightly before letting her go. Climbing on to Nomis, he faced the portal and set his shoulders.

Nervousness seized his throat, so he simply waved to the people on the ground, who were backing away to give Nomis room to take off.

Nudging Nomis with his knees, Ben felt the dragon's reluctance to go through as he hesitated to take off. When he did, Nomis turned slowly in the air to get a clear, even shot to the opening of the portal. It flared, as if anticipating the creature about to pass through. Then, they slid past the opening and into the portal itself.

Ben was forced to close his eyes against the brightness of the flare. Then a moment later, he was completely surrounded by the light, which was penetrating his eyelids, making him see red. His lungs felt compressed as he gulped for air. When the intensity finally died down, Ben dared to open his eyes.

Below him, instead of the city, was the familiar stretch of snow, broken only by the distant Slippit Road and a small house. Smiling, Ben kneed Nomis to a slow descent towards the house. A few minutes later, Ben stood on the doorstep of the place he hadn't seen in months.

So much had changed since the last time he was here. He'd been falsely arrested, met an Ice Elf, gotten lost in and escaped from the mountains, been attacked by soldiers, learned to hunt his own dinner, been to a royal ball, and battled the King of Iceworld himself. Ben had changed just as much as his experiences had, and he smiled, looking back over the expanse of snow that he had led a beautiful and distraught girl over less than a year ago.

Sighing heavily, Ben put his hand on the doorknob, twisted it gently, and opened the door slowly.

Ben peeked around the doorframe and saw the enormously slimmed figure of his mother sitting in front of the fire, staring into its depths with black, red eyes. In her hand, she held a picture of Ben and his father together when Ben had been little. It was obvious that she thought Ben had died as well.

When she heard the door creak, she turned in her chair, her eyes bleak. When her eyes focused on Ben, she stood, mouth hanging open, as if she couldn't believe it was him.

"Hi, Mom," he said lamely, waving rather pathetically at the woman so recently mourning his death.

In an instant she was hugging him, tears streaming down her face. "Ben, you're alive! You're safe! Oh, when you didn't come home, I thought... I thought..." She let out a fresh sob, clutching her son to her. "It doesn't matter what I thought. You're home," she wept on his shoulder as he hugged her back, relieved that she was still all right.

Wiping off her tears, she pulled him over to sit down and immediately started fussing over him, trying to fix him something to eat yet eagerly wanting to talk with him. Pausing, she realized something and turned to face him, brandishing a wooden spoon at him.

"What about Mia?" she questioned seriously. "You got her home?"

He stood up and went to kiss his mom on her forehead. Chuckling, Ben grinned as he replied, "Yeah, yeah I did."

ABOUT THE AUTHOR

Katherine Phillips resides in rural northern Michigan, and she can rarely be seen without a notebook and pen in hand. Besides writing, she loves reading, chocolate, the treadmill, music, dogs, and a relaxing day with her family or boyfriend.

Those who enjoyed *Iceworld* may want to follow Mia's reign in *Theros, The Siege of Iceworld*.

Made in the USA
Charleston, SC
29 March 2011